My
OTTER
Half

My OTTER Half

Michelle Schusterman

Scholastic Inc.

For Jordan, the Pacific Northwest's
most majestic Shih Tzu

Copyright © 2022 by Michelle Schusterman
Interior art © Shutterstock.com

All rights reserved. Published by Scholastic Inc., *Publishers since 1920.* SCHOLASTIC and associated logos are trademarks and/or registered trademarks of Scholastic Inc.

The publisher does not have any control over and does not assume any responsibility for author or third-party websites or their content.

ISBN 978-1-338-74149-0

10 9 8 7 6 5 4 3 2 1   22 23 24 25 26

Printed in the U.S.A.   40

First printing, 2022

Book design by Keirsten Geise

1

OLIVER

"Oliver! *Oliver!* **Come look at this!"**

Eagerly, Oliver popped the mussel he'd been cracking open into his mouth, tucked his favorite rock safely under his armpit, and sped up to the surface. His friend Lulu was swimming in circles, occasionally poking her head into the water to urge him on. Pearl and Sammy, two other otter pups who were about a month younger than Oliver, were already there.

Oliver broke the surface and squinted in the bright sunlight. Land was visible in the distance to his left and right, but in front of him, the sea stretched out endlessly.

"What is it?" Oliver asked excitedly, swimming over to Lulu and the others. In response, Lulu pointed behind him. Oliver turned around and gasped.

This strait was pretty wide, but as it grew closer to land—the *big* land, as the otters called it—the waterways grew more and more narrow. At least, that was what Oliver had been told. His mother, Olympia, would never let him swim far enough to see it for himself.

But now, Oliver couldn't see the big land at all. Because a gigantic flatboat was practically taking up the whole strait.

"What is that?" Oliver asked in wonder. "I mean, I know it's a boat, but I've never seen one like *that* before!"

"It's so big!" Pearl exclaimed.

"It's so flat!" Sammy added.

"It's called a tanker," Lulu said importantly. "My momma told me. And this is a small one! Momma brought me way out in the ocean once and we saw one *three times* that size!"

"Wow," Oliver said. As usual, he couldn't help feeling a little jealous. Lulu's mother was always taking Lulu close to land and farther afield to show her interesting things. Whenever he asked Olympia if they could join them, Olympia tsked and shook her head. "It's too risky!" she would say.

"I want to see it up close!" Sammy cried, flapping his tail and splashing the others. "Who's with me?"

Oliver's stomach sank.

"Me, me, me!" Pearl exclaimed. "Let's go!"

"It's really close to the big land now," Lulu said, gazing at the tanker. "Maybe too far for you two."

"Nuh-uh!" Sammy said. "Our momma took us on land already! That island right over there!"

"We played on the beach," Pearl said smugly.

Oliver's mouth fell open. "You did?"

"Sure! You have, too, right, Oliver?"

"Come on, Pearl," Sammy said, giggling. "You know his momma won't let him do anything."

Oliver flushed with embarrassment. "That's not true!"

But it was true. Oliver was a whole month older than Pearl and Sammy, but he'd never been on land. Every time he asked, Olympia had the same response. "Not yet, Ollie. Wait till you're just a little bit older."

"You mean you did it?" Lulu asked, her eyes wide as she gazed at Oliver. "Why didn't you tell me? Which island? What'd you do? What'd you see?"

"I—um—well—" Oliver stuttered. Why had he said that? He was a terrible liar!

Pearl and Sammy started to snicker.

"See? He still hasn't been on land!"

"Aw, Ollie, really?"

"It's not his fault! He's a momma otter's boy!"

"Okay, okay," Lulu said, giving Oliver a sympathetic look. "Oliver will go on land when he's ready."

But her pity made Oliver feel even worse. "I am ready," he said, slapping his paws on the water for emphasis. "I'm *more* than ready. I . . ."

He paused, gazing out at the tanker. It was already almost out of sight, disappearing behind one of the islands across from the big land. Oliver knew where it was headed. All the boats that came from the sea and sailed through the strait went to the same place.

"I'm going to swim to Puget Sound!"

Pearl and Sammy gasped. Lulu's eyes widened. Sea otters never ventured into the Sound. It was a big, complicated system of straits and waterways and basins with lots of islands and *so* many boats and Jet Skis and water skis and swimmers—way too dangerous for otters to try and navigate.

But Oliver couldn't back down now.

"Watch me!" he said, then he dove back underwater and began to swim.

He kicked his back legs and enjoyed the feel of speeding through the water. After a few minutes, he could see the dark, murky shadow of the tanker way up ahead. Oliver grinned to himself, imagining the looks on his friends' faces when he returned. Maybe he'd even bring back a souvenir from the Sound.

"Oliver!"

A white, furry face with black eyes popped up in

front of Oliver so suddenly, he had to do a backflip to avoid crashing into her.

"Momma?!"

"What in the great wide sea do you think you're doing?" Olympia cried, her whiskers twitching. Her voice quivered with worry, and Oliver felt a twinge of guilt.

"I was just swimming, Momma."

"Swimming *where*, exactly?"

"Um . . ." Oliver blinked several times. "Nowhere special."

Sighing, Olympia pulled Oliver up to the surface. They both shook the water out of their eyes. Distant giggling reached Oliver's ears, and he glanced behind him to see Lulu, Sammy, and Pearl poking their heads out of the water. He looked away, ashamed.

They were right. He *was* a momma otter's boy.

"Oliver, tell the truth. Where were you going?"

"I . . ." Oliver swallowed hard. "Just . . . that island over there."

"Oliver!"

"Pearl and Sammy went and played on the beach!" Oliver cried. "They said it was fun and not dangerous at all!"

"We've had this discussion, sweetie," Olympia said with a sigh. "I'll take you to the beach when you're old enough."

"But Pearl and Sammy are younger than me!" Oliver crossed his arms. "And Lulu got to go under that tanker with her momma."

Olympia looked horrified. "Under a *tanker*? Good gracious."

"But nothing bad happened!" Oliver pointed out. "Just like nothing bad happened to Pearl and Sammy on the beach! Can't I just—"

"Oliver, listen." Olympia rose up a few inches out of the water, and Oliver fell silent. "You have to trust me, sweetie. I know what's best for you. And I'll take you to the beach when you're ready. Okay?"

Oliver knew there was no point in arguing. "Okay," he mumbled.

"Good." Olympia pulled Oliver close. He hugged

her back, even though he was still a little bit upset, and a *lot* bit embarrassed. "Now you float right here, and I'll finish fetching our lunch."

She planted a big, wet kiss on his furry cheek, then dove back into the water. Oliver floated on his back and stared up at the sky. He tried to relax, but he could still hear his friends giggling in the distance.

"That does it." Oliver straightened up and stared straight ahead. The tanker was out of sight now, and he could see the big land spread out before him, bright green and beautiful. All he had to do was swim for the big land, then take a right, and he'd be in the Sound. How hard could it be?

Without giving himself a chance to overthink it, Oliver plunged deep into the water and began to swim as fast as his legs could paddle.

2

 **LUCY**

Lucy Carmichael hummed as she browsed the cherry selection at the Kingston farmer's market. Well, she *tried* to browse. It was a little hard to do with the thirty pounds of squirming brown fur in her arms.

"Do you have any Rainiers left?" she asked the smiling woman in the Bernice's Berry Orchard apron.

"I think I might." The woman ducked behind the boxes of shiny red Bing and Chelan cherries. She reappeared a moment later holding a small container. "It's your lucky day!" she said cheerfully. "This is the last of the season."

The sight of the Rainier cherries, bright yellow with a deep pink blush, made Lucy's mouth water. "Thank you!" she said, trying in vain to pull out the five-dollar bill folded up in her pocket. "Just a sec . . . Franklin, hold still!"

The woman's smile widened as Lucy struggled to cling to her overly enthusiastic puppy. "He is *so* cute! Is he a dachshund?"

"Yes!" Lucy finally extracted the bill and handed it over. "He's ten months old." Franklin grinned up at her, his tongue hanging out. One of his long brown ears had flopped back, and his collar had loosened a little and spun around so the tags hung off the side.

"Poor little guy just wants to play," the woman cooed, reaching out and tickling Franklin under the chin. "I just love his little beard!"

"He's extra hyper because he took his first ferry ride today," Lucy explained as the woman tucked the bill into the pocket of her apron. "We live on Whidbey Island."

"Aw, how exciting!" The woman came around the

table to tuck the container of cherries into the tote bag that hung from Lucy's arm. "You know, we've got a great little off-leash dog park right on the water! It's just up that way."

She pointed, and Lucy turned to look at the Sound. Sure enough, she could see a dozen or so furry bodies with wagging tails, all climbing over driftwood or splashing in the water.

"Thank you!" Lucy said, wrapping both arms around a wiggling Franklin and kissing the top of his head. "We'll check it out."

But she walked in the opposite direction of the dog park. Lucy couldn't imagine letting Franklin off the leash. Even *on* the leash he was a handful! He'd practically dislocated Lucy's shoulder the first time he'd seen a squirrel. If she ever let him run free, Lucy was positive Franklin would run for hours before he even realized she wasn't there.

"Lucy! Over here!"

Lucy stood on tiptoe, looking around the crowd milling from booth to booth. Finally, she spotted her mother's auburn hair and bright pink Sound Marine Lab shirt at a coffee kiosk.

"One cold brew, extra cream," said a guy in a backward blue cap, holding out a mason jar filled with coffee. "Bring this jar back when you visit and you get half off any drink!"

"Thanks so much," Mom said before taking a huge sip and turning to Lucy. "Any luck with the cherries?"

"Got the last Rainiers!" Lucy said, hugging Franklin closer as he batted his paws at Mom. "Ouch, Franklin! I think we need to trim your nails."

"Or you could just put him down," Mom said wryly. "Luce, hon, he needs his exercise!"

"I know . . ."

"Here, want me to take his leash?"

"No, that's okay." Reluctantly, Lucy set Franklin down, then wrapped his leash around her hand three times. They began to walk toward the water, the excited puppy yipping and prancing around Lucy's feet.

"I think there's a dog park somewhere around here," Mom suggested. "Why don't we—"

"No way!" Lucy said, her stomach flipping over at the thought. "He's too young, Mom. We're still training him to come when we call him, and he doesn't always do it. What if he runs off and we can't catch him? What if he gets in a fight with another dog?"

Lucy had been taking a training class with Franklin. It was not going well. He followed the commands sometimes, but if he was distracted by something— which happened a *lot*—it was like he couldn't even hear Lucy at all.

Mom sighed. "Okay, okay. But let's give him a good walk before we get back in the car, all right? It's going to be a long wait for the ferry."

"Okay," Lucy agreed.

The wind whipped her hair out of its ponytail as they strolled down the pier. Lucy took a deep breath, enjoying the briny, salty seawater smell. It was an unusually cloudless day, and she could see the snow-capped Olympic mountain range in the distance.

Franklin spotted a few seagulls and lunged so hard that Lucy stumbled several steps before regaining her balance.

Mom laughed. "Here, give me a turn!" she said, and this time, Lucy handed the leash over. She giggled as Mom jogged ahead, struggling not to spill her coffee as Franklin pumped his short legs as fast as he could.

Shaking out her sore hand, Lucy walked up to the railing and gazed out at the water. A girl on a Jet Ski soared past, and farther north toward Whidbey Island, Lucy could see a tanker moving slowly but steadily into the Sound. There were a ton of sailboats out today, and a red-and-white whale-watching boat with ABZ TOURS painted on the side . . . *Oh.*

Lucy stood up straight, her heart suddenly pounding. She grabbed the railing and leaned out as far as she dared, her eyes scanning the people on the boat. They were too far away for her to see their faces, but—there. At the front of the boat. A flash of familiar auburn hair.

Zach.

Lucy's big brother had graduated from high school in May. The last time she'd seen him had been the day after the ceremony, when he'd walked out of the house with a backpack and a suitcase without looking back.

Things had been totally normal last fall, as far as Lucy could tell. Seventh grade was a lot more fun than sixth, mostly because Lucy had joined her school's videography club. Mom surprised her with Franklin for her birthday in November. Zach seemed to be having a great senior year, and he got accepted to four universities. Everything had been perfect.

But after the holidays, Zach surprised everyone by telling Mom that he didn't want to go to college. That's when everything had gone south.

At first, Lucy thought Zach was being ridiculous. Why wouldn't he want to go to college? What was he going to do, lounge around and play video games all day? She sat silently at the dinner table night after night, too anxious to eat as Mom and Zach argued.

Then one day over spring break, Lucy and Zach had taken Franklin for a walk along the beach, and she'd finally asked her brother what in the world he was thinking.

"I don't need a degree to do what I want to do," Zach had told her, throwing a large, flat rock way out in the water. "I get where Mom's coming from, but there's no point in waiting four years to start my business."

"What business?" Lucy asked, baffled.

Zach's eyes lit up. "Me and Alex and Bryson are starting an adventure tour company! Kayaking, hiking, river rafting, whale watching . . ."

And he'd launched into a lengthy description of how the business would work. Lucy had listened, her confusion turning to enthusiasm—and admiration. Zach had obviously already put a lot of work and thought into this. He and his friends had started working on their plan last summer. And Zach was so *excited* about it. It was hard not to feel excited for him.

But clearly, Mom felt differently.

The arguments had only gotten worse as summer drew closer. Lucy didn't dare take Zach's side in front of Mom, even though she secretly thought his company was an awesome idea. But she couldn't help but wish Zach would at least try to see Mom's side of it, too. Sometimes it seemed like he was *trying* to pick a fight with her. And neither of them noticed how anxious their arguing made Lucy. The tension in the house was unbearable all through May, and when Zach finally stormed out for good, it was almost a relief.

Except Lucy missed her big brother terribly. He still texted her every day, and they video chatted every once in a while. But that wasn't the same as seeing him in person. It wasn't like he'd moved to another state—she knew he was staying with his friend Alex in Edmonds, which wasn't *that* far from Whidbey. But Zach's anger at Mom was apparently bigger than his desire to hang out with his little sister.

Which hurt Lucy's feelings, if she was being honest. But at least Zach was happy now. And Lucy didn't have to hide in her bedroom and watch YouTube videos with the volume all the way up to drown out all the yelling.

"This little dude can run!"

Lucy jumped, startled, as Mom appeared at her side. She was panting almost as hard as Franklin, whose little tongue lolled out to the side.

"Mom, look at that tanker!" Lucy said, her voice coming out strangely high-pitched. Mom handed her the leash and wiped the sweat from her forehead as she turned to look in the opposite direction of the ABZ Tours boat. Lucy held the leash loosely, her hands shaking slightly. She didn't want Mom to see Zach.

"Franklin, sit," she said, and the puppy planted his back end on the pier. "Stay."

The one and only time Lucy had dared to bring up Zach this summer had been when the new season of *Skywriter*, the only show all three of them loved, had come out in July. Lucy and Mom had watched the first few episodes together, but it wasn't the same without Zach's sarcastic commentary. Later that night, she'd heard Mom crying in her bedroom.

"I see it," Mom said, gazing at the tanker. "Hey, can I have a few of those cherries?"

"Sure!" Lucy glanced nervously at Zach's boat as she rummaged in her tote bag. It was farther away now, but she could still see his auburn hair. "Here you go. Franklin, I have something for you, too!" Lucy pulled out a little bag of gourmet dog treats she'd bought at the market. "Here you . . ."

Lucy trailed off, staring down at the leash. Which was connected to Franklin's collar. Which was lying on the pier.

And Franklin was nowhere to be seen.

3

 **FRANKLIN**

Squirrel.

Squirrel.

SQUIRREL!

Franklin veered off the pier and tore up a rocky path leading to a thicket of trees. His gaze was locked on to the thick, fluffy tail up ahead. Franklin didn't understand why the squirrel was running. Squirrels *always* ran from Franklin. All he wanted was to ask them a few hundred questions and maybe see if they'd teach him how to climb a tree. But they were all so skittish! Maybe if he barked at it, the squirrel would stop running.

"Arf! *Arf!*"

The squirrel put on a fresh burst of speed and tore up a tree, vanishing into the canopy of leaves overhead. Franklin put his paws on the trunk and gazed up eagerly, waiting for it to reappear.

It didn't.

Franklin dropped to all fours, only mildly disappointed. That was the closest he'd ever come to catching a squirrel. Maybe next time he just needed to bark louder.

Now, where was Lucy? Franklin lifted his snout and took a good, long sniff. The water wasn't too far away. His ears pricked up as he heard the distant sounds of people at the farmer's market. As Franklin began trotting down the path, he realized it was too quiet. The jingle sound was missing. His tags—his collar, his leash! How did *that* happen? Franklin remembered running up and down the pier with Lucy's mom, and then Lucy told him to sit and he sat, and she told him to stay, and then . . . *squirrel.*

Anytime Franklin spotted a squirrel, the whole world sort of went fuzzy.

He hoped Lucy wasn't too worried. She'd kept such a tight grip on him all day. And while Franklin loved being cuddled, sometimes he could feel all the energy building up inside him until he thought he'd *burst*. Today was definitely one of those days.

When Franklin reached the edge of the thicket, he heard a light rustling not far behind him. He spun around and spotted a fluffy brown tail.

Squirrel!

"ARF-ARF-ARF!"

Franklin took off, sprinting after the squirrel as fast as he could.

Nearly an hour later, Franklin finally started to feel a little bit tired. Today had been the best day *ever*. Sure, he hadn't caught the squirrel, but he'd tracked it deep into the woods, where he'd picked up so many other interesting scents. He'd lapped extra-cold water out of a stream filled with shiny silver fish, and he'd seen all sorts of birds, and he'd relieved himself on the side of a gigantic tree. It was all so exciting!

Now, he was letting his nose guide him to the beach. But the moment Franklin's paws touched the pebbles, he knew this wasn't where he was supposed to be. Yes, there was the water. But there were no tents, no people, no pier. This was a smaller beach, with more rocks than sand, and it was covered in smooth, white logs.

Franklin yawned. He knew he should keep looking for Lucy, but he really was getting sleepy now. Besides, Lucy always found him. She was *very* good at hide-and-seek.

This was as good a place to wait for her to find him as any, right?

Franklin spotted a nice, thick stick and picked it up. It was a little bit damp and tasted like the sea. He settled down next to one of the white logs and began gnawing on his stick.

Way out in the water, he spotted a big, flat boat. *Why was it so flat?* Franklin wondered sleepily. If he could catch the boat, he would ask it. But that would mean swimming. And while Franklin would happily run all day long, he wasn't too fond of swimming.

Lucy took him to the beach near their house all the time, and Franklin loved splashing around in the water that lapped up onto the shore. But actually *swimming*? Going way, way out into the ocean and letting the waves take over and push you this way and that? No thanks.

By the time the flat boat was passing his little beach, Franklin's eyes were beginning to droop. He abandoned his stick and settled his head on his paws. Was the boat supposed to be turning like that? It was still moving with the current, but the front was pointed more toward Franklin. That didn't seem right. If only Franklin could just *ask* the boat.

The sun was setting behind the mountains, and Franklin's eyelids were so, so heavy. He tried to keep watching, but before long he slipped into a deep sleep.

His dreams were filled with squirrels. He didn't catch any of them, either.

When Franklin woke up, his first thought was wondering why the foot of Lucy's bed was covered in rocks.

Then he opened his eyes. Then he bolted upright.

The farmer's market. The pier. The squirrel. The tanker. Franklin remembered all of it. Only now, it didn't feel like such a fun adventure. Fun adventures always ended with him curled up at the foot of Lucy's bed. Not sleeping out here in the wild—and so close to the water, too! Franklin shivered. Thank goodness he hadn't gotten soaked in his sleep.

It was very early in the morning, and the seagulls were making a racket. Out in the water, the tanker Franklin had watched last night was drifting in a slow, lazy circle. Waves lapped onto the shore, and a strange shadow was sliding up onto the rocks and the logs, creeping closer and closer to Franklin. He blinked, shook his head extra hard, and looked again. No, that wasn't a shadow.

The water was *black*.

4

 **OLIVER**

Why had Oliver ever thought this was a good idea?

He'd been swimming for what felt like hours and still wasn't anywhere near land. He didn't care about impressing Lulu and Pearl and Sammy anymore. All he wanted was a nice juicy crab lunch and then a good long nap.

It wasn't just that he was tired, though. Oliver hated to admit it, even to himself, but an uneasiness had been creeping over him for the last hour or so. He wasn't sure why—maybe it was the lack of marine life in this part of the ocean—but something just felt *off*.

Either that, or maybe he really was just a momma otter's boy after all.

The next time Oliver surfaced, he realized with a start that the sky had gone from blue to pink. The sun was setting! He really had been gone a long time. Momma must be so worried about him. The thought made his tummy twist with guilt.

When Oliver dove back beneath the waves, he barely saw the massive school of fish coming in time to dodge out of their way.

"Hey, what's the rush?" he called, but none of the silvery fish spared him a response. They looked focused—in fact, they almost looked frightened. Oliver glanced around. Maybe a shark or some other predator was nearby? But he didn't see anything that was cause for alarm.

Oliver started to swim, when suddenly a sea lion sped by not too far away. This time, it wasn't Oliver's imagination: The sea lion looked *scared*.

Oliver's heart began to pound. He'd never seen a scared sea lion before. They were some of the bravest animals he knew. "What's going on?" he said, but the sea lion either didn't hear him or pretended not to.

That's it, Oliver decided. *I'm going home.*

He set off in the opposite direction, only the current was too strong and he could barely move forward. Oliver dropped a little lower. The water was darker here, and with night quickly falling, it was getting harder and harder to see. Oliver had just begun to paddle again, when—*SLAM!*

"Ouch!" he cried, tumbling to the side as a massive, spotted gray creature with big black eyes and a black nose clipped him.

Whoosh! Whoosh! Whoosh! Whoosh! Whoosh!

Oliver gaped as five seals streamed past him. The one that had accidentally knocked into him with her fin spotted him and turned, slowing down long enough to call out:

"Better get out of here fast, kid! Hurry up, now!"

"What? Why?" Oliver said, but she was already catching up with her pod.

If Oliver had been unsettled before, now he was

well and truly frightened. Was there a whale? Every once in a while, a whale made its way into Puget Sound. But no, that couldn't be it—sea lions and seals didn't flee from whales like that. Oliver glanced behind him as he began to swim after the seals . . . then he did a double take.

There *was* something behind him. Something even bigger than a whale, and much, much more ominous.

Oliver had seen a squid release a plume of ink once. The black ink had billowed out in the water like a rolling cloud, expanding wider and wider until fading away.

Now, he thought he might be looking at an ink cloud released by the biggest squid in the whole entire world.

Only that couldn't be it. Because while this massive cloud of black was expanding—and rapidly—it wasn't fading away. If anything, it was only getting thicker and darker as it grew.

The pit of fear in Oliver's tummy bloomed into full-on terror. He sped after the seals, not daring to look back at the black cloud. But he could sense it closing in, and fast.

"Oliver! *Oliver!*"

"Momma?" Oliver gasped. He swam even harder, listening hard as her voice grew louder and louder. There was the pod of seals, and there were more sea lions, and turtles, and a porpoise and crabs and so, *so* many fish. Oliver realized they were all approaching the entrance to the strait—the last narrow part of the Sound before it opened up to the ocean. Every single living creature in Puget Sound was racing to the sea, and the strait was total chaos.

"Momma? Momma!" Oliver cried again and again, but he couldn't hear her anymore. There were too many creatures speeding by, and he couldn't keep up. He didn't dare look back at that awful black cloud. Oliver wanted to cry as he swam as hard as he could. And suddenly—

"Oliver!"

When Olympia's white furry face popped up in front of Oliver, he went weak with relief.

"Momma! I'm sorry, I'm really sorry—"

"Not now! Just hurry!" Olympia didn't seem angry as she pulled Oliver through the water. She looked scared. And not like when Oliver stayed underwater too long, or asked if he could go closer to the beach, or strayed too close to a pelican.

No, this was *real* fear in Olympia's large black eyes.

"What's going on?" Oliver asked desperately as they swam.

But Olympia didn't answer. The strait was crowded with marine life now, and Oliver stuck close to his momma's side as they darted past a slow-moving jellyfish. Then, out of nowhere—

SMACK!

Something hard slammed into Oliver, sending him spiraling away from Olympia. He barely caught a glimpse of a sea turtle hurtling past at astonishing speed before he was surrounded by tiny, frantically flitting yellow fish.

"Momma!" he yelled, swatting at the fish and trying to see. He thought he heard Olympia calling his name, but he couldn't even tell which direction her voice was coming from. Oliver grunted, twisting and turning and finally escaping the chaotic school of fish and getting a better look at his surroundings.

"Oliver?"

He looked up. "Momma?"

A few more sea lions swam past, and Oliver got caught up in their current. He flipped head over tail several times and finally landed, dizzy and disoriented, on the sandy ocean floor.

Oliver rubbed his head and looked around. The last few seals were visible in the distance, disappearing into the dusky water. Suddenly, he was alone.

Only, he wasn't alone. Oliver could sense something coming up behind him, fast.

He turned slowly, his heart pounding hard in his chest. The giant wall of black was racing toward him way, way too fast. Oliver tried to swim away, paddling as hard as his limbs could paddle, but it was no use.

In seconds, the blackness swallowed him up.

 **LUCY**

Riiiiiiing! Riiiiiiing!

Lucy's hand darted out from under her blanket. She groped blindly for her phone, wondering why the alarm tone had changed from the guitar strumming she'd chosen months ago to this shrill, electronic ringing.

Blearily, she opened her eyes and stared at her screen. The time read 6:23 a.m., and her alarm wasn't going off.

The ringing had stopped. Lucy lay there, half wanting to go back to sleep. But a sense of panic was starting to settle over her, and distantly she thought she really needed to get up because there was something *wrong* . . . but what?

Sighing, Lucy sat up and nudged Franklin with her toes, the way she did every morning.

Only Franklin wasn't curled up in his usual spot by her feet.

And suddenly, the awful memory of yesterday came rushing back. Looking down and realizing she was holding a leash with a collar attached, but no puppy.

Mom had stayed calm. "He can't have gotten far," she reassured Lucy, before taking off down the pier to look for him. Lucy had sprinted in the opposite direction, trying to take comfort in Mom's words. But she couldn't. Because the thing was, Lucy knew in her gut that Mom was wrong.

Franklin *could* have gotten far. He was so, so fast! In just a few seconds, he could vanish from sight. That was why Lucy always kept such a tight grip on him. But she'd been distracted by the sight of Zach's whale-watching boat out on the water, and she hadn't

noticed Franklin slipping out of his collar and speeding off to . . . to *where*?

Lucy and Mom had stayed at the farmer's market
until the sky was the color of pink grapefruit and the
sun hovered just over the mountain peaks. They called
Franklin's name over and over until Lucy's throat was
hoarse. They asked anyone who would listen if they'd
seen him, and Lucy would hold up the most recent
photo of Franklin on her phone. Finally, a young
woman with a silver stud in her nose and thick, wavy
black hair swept up into a high ponytail had nodded
in recognition.

"Oh yeah, I did see that little guy! He was chasing
a squirrel right over there."

She pointed, and for a moment, Lucy's heart soared.
Then she saw the woman was gesturing to a path that
led into the woods.

"When was that?" Mom had asked, and the woman
frowned thoughtfully.

"Half an hour ago, maybe?"

Lucy and Mom had walked the path until it

started to get dark. But Lucy knew it was hopeless. If Franklin was chasing a squirrel, he'd been running *fast*. There was no way they'd find him now.

She'd sobbed the entire car ride home. Mom did her best to comfort her.

"It's entirely possible someone found him," she said, pulling into the driveway. "And if that's the case, I'm sure we'll be getting a phone call soon!"

"B-but he's not wearing his collar!" Lucy wailed, holding up the collar, which was still attached to the leash. "How will they know who he b-belongs to?"

"He has a chip, remember?" Mom gave Lucy a bracing smile as she turned off the engine. "The vet did it at his last appointment. If someone finds him, all they have to do is take him to a shelter or a vet, and they'll scan his chip and get all our information."

Lucy hiccuped and nodded, too miserable to respond. She'd stayed up way too late making a MISS-ING DOG sign and printing dozens of copies. Then, at last, she'd managed to fall into an uneasy sleep.

Rubbing her eyes, Lucy listened to the muffled

sound of her mother's voice coming from the living room. Suddenly, she remembered what Mom had said.

The chip! Maybe someone had found Franklin and gotten his chip scanned!

Throwing off her blankets, Lucy hurtled out of her room. She passed the empty room next to hers—the one Zach used to live in—and skidded to a halt in the living room. Mom stood by the windows, her back to Lucy, one hand on her hip and the other holding the phone to her ear. Lucy fidgeted, longing to ask if the call was about Franklin, but not wanting to interrupt.

Outside, the sky was flamingo pink and streaked with tiny white clouds. Lucy could see the snowy caps of the mountains in the distance, barely visible over the tops of the fir trees in their backyard. The signs she'd made last night were stacked neatly on the coffee table. A black-and-white photo of Franklin, sitting up straight with his head slightly tilted and his tongue lolling out over his beard, caused a painful tugging in

Lucy's heart. She tore her gaze away and looked back at the windows.

After a moment, Mom turned around. She was nodding, listening to whoever was on the other end. But her expression instantly put Lucy on edge.

Whatever this call was about, it wasn't someone who'd found Franklin safe and sound. Something was wrong.

After what felt like an eternity, Mom finally said, "Got it. I'll be there soon." She hung up, and Lucy couldn't stop the words from tumbling out.

"Is it Franklin? Did someone . . . did they find him?"

"Oh, sweetie." Mom's expression cleared, and she hurried forward to give Lucy a hug. "That wasn't about Franklin at all, honey."

Relief swept through Lucy, quickly followed by devastation. No news was definitely not *good* news. "What's wrong, then?"

She waited for Mom to tell her nothing was wrong, everything was fine. That was what Mom always did.

Unless something was *very* wrong.

Mom sighed, pinching the bridge of her nose. "That was Emily, at the lab. There was an oil spill in Puget Sound last night."

Lucy's stomach dropped. "Oh," she whispered. She'd seen videos of oil spills before, and she knew a few had happened in the Pacific Northwest. Never so close to home, though. "Is it bad?"

"It's relatively small. And they already have it contained—the tanker isn't leaking anymore, which is excellent. But still, there's going to be a lot of damage, and the local wildlife is in danger," Mom went on, moving into the kitchen. Lucy followed her, although she couldn't imagine eating breakfast at a time like this. "That's obviously going to be our first priority. Honey, I know I promised I'd help you look for Franklin today, but—"

"It's okay, I understand," Lucy said immediately. Her puppy was lost, it was true. But hundreds—maybe even thousands—of animals were in trouble right now. "I want to help, too. Can I come?"

Glancing up from the coffee pot, Mom smiled for the first time that morning. "Oh, honey. That'd be great. The more hands on deck, the better."

"I'll go get dressed," Lucy said, already heading for the door.

"Jeans and a long-sleeved shirt! I know it's pretty warm out, but we're going to have to cover up for this."

"Got it!" Lucy called back. Before going back to her bedroom to get ready, she went to the coffee table in the living room and gathered up the flyers she'd made about Franklin.

She had every intention of helping Mom save the animals. But that didn't mean she couldn't do whatever she could to find Franklin, too.

6

 **FRANKLIN**

Franklin felt uneasy. Maybe it was the black water. Maybe it was the fact that he'd spent the night outside alone for the first time in his whole life. Whatever the reason, he didn't like feeling this way. He needed to do something to feel normal and happy again.

So he decided to take himself on a walk.

It wasn't as fun without Lucy. She would always giggle when he'd pick up a stick that was just a little too big for him, or when he just had to stop and sniff at every pine cone or snail or pretty much anything they passed.

But Franklin had to admit, it was super fun to just

follow his nose and not worry about Lucy tugging the leash and pulling him back.

They never walked anywhere that was covered in all this slick black stuff. Franklin had been trotting down a quiet little bay for most of the morning, and the black stuff was *everywhere*. Every time a gentle wave lapped onto shore, it left behind more of the weird goo—it coated the pebbles, the rocks, the driftwood. Franklin could feel it sticking to the bottom of his paws.

He didn't much like the chemical smell of the stuff. And he definitely didn't like the slimy feel of it. But he really liked the bay, and besides, it was by the water. He'd left Lucy and her mom close to the water. Surely they must be close by. Lucy had never taken this long with hide-and-seek before.

Franklin wondered if Lucy was worried about him. She seemed to worry a lot in general. He felt bad at the thought.

And though he wasn't quite ready to admit it to himself, he felt a teeny, tiny bit worried, too.

Spotting the slow, steady crawl of a hermit crab near a bone-white chunk of driftwood, Franklin charged forward. Then another movement caught his eye.

Squirrel?

He turned sharply and froze, tail sticking straight out. It wasn't a squirrel, that much he could tell right away. But there was a creature of some sort, around Franklin's size, stirring next to a giant rock. It looked like it had taken a bath in the black goo. Franklin's whiskers twitched, and he moved closer.

The creature had fallen suspiciously still. Sleeping, Franklin realized with relief when it let out a tiny snore. Beneath the layer of black goo, he saw the creature had brown fur, just like him! Surely it hadn't taken a bath in that stinky, mucky stuff on purpose?

Not that Franklin would judge it if it had. Personally, he loved rolling around in the mud. The last time it had rained, Franklin had managed to squirm out of Lucy's arms before the back door had closed. He'd made a beeline straight for a nice, smelly mud puddle.

Lucy had charged outside yelling at him to come back inside. But once she'd seen him rolling around on his back, his stubby legs flailing in the air, she'd started laughing really hard, and Franklin knew she wasn't actually mad at him.

But that was *mud*. Mud was great.

This black stuff was definitely not mud, and Franklin had no desire to be covered in it.

And the closer he got to this creature, the more he thought it hadn't been rolling around happily in the goo before falling asleep. Its fur was matted and knotted, and the black goo was stuck to its nostrils and its eyes and its whiskers. The creature had paws—just like Franklin!—and it was hard to see the nails thanks to all the goo. The creature also had a tail, but it was *not* like Franklin's tail. It was oddly flat, like it had been smashed. Only Franklin didn't think it had actually been smashed. It was just a super flat tail.

Was this a dog? Franklin had met other dogs before, and he knew they didn't all look alike. This maybe-dog looked a lot more like Franklin than Juno, the gigantic dog who lived next door to Lucy. Juno was gray and white and had legs so long that when she stood up on her back legs, she was taller than Lucy! Their neighbor said Juno was a Great Dane, and Franklin thought that was a very appropriate name for such an enormous dog.

Then there was Rogue, who belonged to Lucy's mom's friend Ellen. Rogue was also bigger than Franklin, but not nearly as big as Juno. She had pretty striped fur and pointy ears, and when she grinned it took up pretty much her entire head. Ellen said Rogue was a pit bull. Rogue only had three legs, but even so, she could still run way, way faster than Franklin.

Franklin knew he was a dachshund, because Lucy was quick to inform everyone they met. He wondered how many different types of dogs there were.

And if this creature was indeed a dog, what type of dog was it?

A fantastic thought struck Franklin. This dog looked as though it had been swimming in the blackened waters. What if it *lived* there? What if it was some sort of *sea* dog? *A sea dachshund?* How amazing would that be?

Franklin knew what he had to do. He had to get a sniff. Smells told Franklin so much more about dogs (and people, and everything, really) than sight or sound did.

He crept closer and closer, not wanting to startle the sea dachshund. Slowly, he leaned forward until they were nose to nose.

SNIIIIIIIIIIIIFF!

Franklin tried to be quiet about it, but his nose whistled a little bit. The sea dachshund didn't move, though.

And it wasn't a sea dachshund. Franklin felt a little disappointed as his mind sorted through all the scents. Whatever this creature was, it wasn't any type of dog at all.

Suddenly, its eyes flew open and it let out a piercing squeak!

"Arf! Arf! Arf! Arf! Arf!"

Franklin leaped away, but he couldn't stop barking.

This always happened when something startled him, like a knock at the door or a *thump* in the next room or a bird tapping on the other side of the window while Franklin napped on the couch. Lucy would clamp her hands over her ears and her mom would call Franklin's name over and over, but once the barking started, he could *not* control it.

Clearly, the creature was just as alarmed as Franklin. It scrambled away, then started trying to climb up the rock. But the black goo was all over the rock, too, and the surface was shiny and slick, and the creature kept slipping and sliding down every few inches.

"Arf-arf-arf! Arf-arf-arf!"

Franklin switched from his alarm bark to his warning bark—but it was no good. Franklin yelped as the creature slipped right off the rock and began to fall!

7

 **OLIVER**

Oliver landed hard on his back and stared up at the sky, dazed. He had never been so exhausted, so frightened, and so alone in his entire life. Everything that had happened yesterday felt like a bad dream.

At first, he swam hard through the black water. But before long, it grew harder and harder to move. The water felt thick and sludgy in a way he'd never experienced, and it was only getting worse. It didn't matter which direction he chose.

He couldn't call out for Momma. He opened his mouth once, and that was enough—a slick, slimy substance coated his mouth and throat, and he kept his mouth clamped shut tight after that.

Finally, he gave up trying to swim and allowed the current to take him wherever it wanted.

"It'll take you to land, if you give it long enough," Lulu had told him once. "My momma says the water takes *everything* to the land eventually. Unless it's really, really heavy."

Oliver was not really, really heavy. But he was starting to feel like maybe he was. Whatever this awful black stuff was, it coated him and weighed him down in a way he did not like one bit.

His eyelids began to droop, but he couldn't sleep. What if he just drifted to the bottom of the sea? Oliver forced himself to stay awake until finally, after what must have been hours, his paws grazed sand.

Coughing and sputtering, Oliver allowed the gentle waves to wash him onto the shore. Then he clambered to a pile of rocks where the water didn't reach and slipped into a deep, dreamless sleep.

Hours later, he felt the warmth of the early morning sun on his face. But something was terribly wrong.

First of all, he felt like he was wearing an extra layer of skin.

Second of all, something cold and wet was touching his nose. And *sniffing*.

Oliver's eyes flew open, and he found himself staring into a pair of wide brown eyes. He scrambled away with a shout—only something was wrong with his throat, and it came out more like a shriek instead. (He was very, very glad Sammy and Pearl weren't around to hear that!)

A brown, furry creature about Oliver's size began to *bark*. Petrified, Oliver attempted to scramble up the rock. The only creatures he'd ever heard bark before were sea lions. But this was no sea lion. He had no idea what it was, but it sounded frantic.

But while Oliver was usually pretty good at climbing, he couldn't seem to make it up the rock. Every few seconds, he'd slip and slide back down. Oliver tried again and again, and the creature barked even more incessantly—and Oliver had fallen.

The creature finally, *finally* fell silent. Oliver lay there, grateful for the peace and quiet. Then he realized he was lying in black sludge.

Was this what land was like? All slick and slippery and stinky? This couldn't have been what Lulu raved about when she came back from her land adventures. Pearl and Sammy had said it was so much fun, too, but this wasn't fun at all.

And they'd never, ever mentioned meeting a . . . a whatever that creature was.

Rolling over, Oliver stared at the furry brown thing. It kind of looked like an otter but with huge, ridiculous flaps on either side of its head. Were those its ears? Why were they so big? Could it hear what was happening on the other side of the world?

Oliver decided this must all be a bad dream after all.

"Momma?" he called, but it came out like a gurgle, and he started to cough uncontrollably. He spit out a gob of black slimy stuff and made a face. What *was* that?

Looking away from the furry thing with the ridiculous ears, Oliver stared out at the water. It lapped onto the beach, leaving smears of more black stuff behind. Oliver's gaze traveled out over the water . . . then landed on the tanker.

Oliver knew with sudden certainty that this was where all the icky black sludge was coming from. He remembered the frantic race through the strait, so many sea creatures swimming as fast as they could, the panicked look on Momma's face as she'd pulled Oliver along . . .

. . . and the sea turtle knocking into them, sending Oliver tumbling away from Momma.

Where was she now? Oliver's heart beat faster. Momma wouldn't have kept going without him. She would have stayed in the strait and looked for him. Which meant she had been swept up in the giant black cloud, too.

Was she here, on this bay? Oliver sat up to look around.

"Are you okay?" the creature asked.

Oliver didn't respond. He was definitely not okay. Nothing was okay.

The furry thing took a tentative step forward. Up close, Oliver could see it had some of the black goo on its paws, and a smudge on its nose. But it was otherwise very clean—and very dry. So it definitely wasn't an otter. Not that Oliver had ever seen an otter with ears like that.

"I think so," he croaked in response. "Do you know what this goo is?"

When he spoke, the furry thing's long, skinny tail went *swish swish swish* back and forth. "Nope! No idea. But I think maybe it came from that giant boat out there."

"It's called a tanker," Oliver said importantly. "It's a . . . well, it's a giant boat, like you said. And you're right. It's where the black stuff came from. I know because I saw it in the water."

"You were in the water?" Franklin looked terribly impressed.

Oliver nodded. "I was trying to swim to Puget Sound, but then this . . . this giant black sort of cloud appeared and it kept growing bigger and bigger."

"Why were you in the water?" Franklin asked eagerly. "Do you live there? How do you breathe? How fast can you swim? I went swimming once. Well, sort of. Lucy brought me into a pool but I did *not* like it at all. I don't like getting wet, no offense . . ."

His rambling was a little overwhelming. But Oliver could tell that this animal, whatever it was, was nice and perfectly harmless.

"No offense taken," he replied. "And yes, I live in the water. I'm an otter. I can swim really, *really* fast!" This was maybe a little bit of an exaggeration, but he figured Franklin didn't need to know that. "This is actually the first time I've ever been on land."

"Wow!" Franklin exclaimed. "Too bad it looks like this."

He gestured at the black slime.

Oliver shuddered. "Believe me, it looks worse in the water. Besides, I didn't actually come here on purpose. I was trying to get away from the black stuff, but it swallowed me up. I was with my momma, but then we . . ."

Suddenly, a lump rose up in Oliver's throat. Franklin's tail stopped wagging, and he tilted his head to one side.

"You haven't seen another otter around here, have you?" Oliver asked hopefully, trying not to cry. "Much bigger than me, brown with a white face?"

Franklin shook his head. "You're the first otter I've ever seen in my whole entire life."

Oliver felt deflated. "Oh. Okay."

"But I can help you look for her!" Franklin said.

"Really?"

"Yeah!" Franklin eyed Oliver. "Although maybe first we should try and get that black stuff off you."

"How? The water's all black, too!"

Franklin looked thoughtful. Then his face broke into a grin. "I know! Follow me!"

He trotted across the bay, and Oliver did his best to keep up. Of all the different ways he'd imagined visiting land for the first time, none of them had been like this at *all*.

"I bet Lucy could help us find your momma," Franklin said as they walked. "She's really, really good at hide-and-seek."

"Is Lucy your momma?" Oliver asked.

"No! She's my . . . my . . ." Franklin seemed to struggle for words. "My girl."

"Girl?" Oliver stared at him in disbelief. "You mean like a *human* girl?"

"Yeah!" Franklin said cheerfully. "She feeds me and plays with me and takes care of me."

Oliver was completely mystified by this revelation. "If you don't mind me asking, what *are* you, anyway? You kind of look like an otter."

"I'm a dachshund." Franklin lifted his head a bit. "That's a type of dog. There are lots of types of dogs. Lucy says I'm the best type."

"Oh." Oliver had more questions—*so* many more—but a glint of gray shell had caught his eye, and he froze in his tracks. A clam was up ahead, making its way across the pebbles, and Oliver had just realized something very important.

He was *starving*!

Instinctively, he reached for the rock in his under-arm pouch. The pouch was all sticky and filled with black sludge, and it was a moment before he realized the awful truth.

"My rock! It's *gone*!"

"What rock?" Franklin asked.

Oliver kept patting his underarm pouch. "You know," he began, then realized Franklin did *not* know, because Franklin was not an otter. "It's a special rock. *My* rock. I've had it since before I can remember. All otters have a special rock. We keep them under here and use them to break open clams and stuff."

He showed Franklin the pouch. Franklin glanced around at the pebbly beach.

"Can't you just use another rock?"

Oliver sighed. "It's not the same." He couldn't find the words to explain to Franklin that his rock was more than just a rock. It was special. Momma had given it to him when he was a baby and he'd used it to crack open every clam and crab he'd ever eaten. Otters carried their special rocks with them their whole lives. Momma had had hers since she was a baby, too. His rock was slanted, sharp on one end and flat on the other, and not so smooth that he couldn't get a good grip on it.

It was *perfect*. And now it was just another thing he'd lost.

Oliver's eyes swam with tears, and he blinked them away. He really did not want to cry in front of Franklin, who was watching him with a very concerned expression.

"I never should have run away," Oliver said, sitting down on the pebbles with a groan. "This is all my fault."

"Run away?" Franklin repeated. "What's that?"

"I wanted to have an adventure," Oliver told him. "I'd never been to land before because my momma said I wasn't old enough and it was too dangerous. But I thought I'd be fine! I always meant to go back home but now I'm just . . . lost."

As he said it, a sad, empty feeling spread through his chest. Oliver had been so preoccupied with the black stuff contaminating the water, he hadn't even considered the fact that he had no idea where he was. Even if he could dive back into the water, he would have no idea which direction was home!

"Uh-oh," Franklin said, and Oliver looked at him. "I think I accidentally ran away, too!"

Whatever Oliver had been expecting him to say, it wasn't that. "You did?"

"Yeah." Franklin sat on his haunches, his back right leg jutting out to the side. "Lucy and I were on the pier with her mom. I was on my leash, of course, but—"

"Leash? What's that?"

"It's a rope that attaches to my collar."

"Collar?"

"That's the thing that goes around my neck. When we go on walks, Lucy holds on to the leash so we stick close together."

Oliver thought this sounded extremely unpleasant.

But saying so would probably be rude, so he kept it to himself.

"Lucy was holding the leash, and she told me to *stay*, but then I . . ." Franklin paused, his eyes going wide and unfocused. "I saw a squirrel. And you know how *that* is."

Oliver did not at all know how—or what—that was.

"I had to chase it! I had to!" Franklin said. "I didn't mean to get out of my collar, but it must've been loose! I was running and running and running and the squirrel got away and when I finally stopped, I didn't see Lucy anywhere. I thought we were just playing hide-and-seek, but . . . maybe I ran away."

"It sounds like you did," Oliver said sympathetically. The sun had risen a bit higher, and the icky black gunk on his fur was getting unpleasantly warm.

His stomach growled again, louder this time.

To his surprise, Franklin's stomach growled right back!

Franklin leaped to his feet. "It's breakfast time!"

He looked around eagerly, tail wagging. Then it drooped. "Aw. For a second there, I thought maybe Lucy was coming. She always brings me breakfast. Oh well. I bet I can find some!"

Oliver watched, bewildered, as Franklin began sniff-sniff-sniffing the ground. His ridiculous ears flattened back against his head, and his tail stuck straight out behind him. It was as if his entire body was focused on sniffing.

At last, he stopped and looked up.

"You said you like clams, right?" Franklin said. When Oliver nodded, he grinned. "There's a whole bunch of them this way!"

With that, the dog charged off in the *opposite* direction of the water!

Oliver followed at a distance, more confused than ever. Clams didn't live on land. Everyone knew that. And how would Franklin even know where they were? Surely he couldn't have smelled them. Oliver took a good, long whiff of the air, but all he smelled was the stinky black goo matted on his fur.

They made their way onto the grass, and then over a hill. Lulu had told Oliver all about grass and hills from her adventures on land. She'd even brought back a pretty yellow thing called a flower, but Oliver didn't see any of those around.

"Ta-da!" Franklin said at last. Oliver saw he was looking at a pink-and-blue shack with tables outside and chairs stacked up against the wall.

Mystified, he followed Franklin around to the back of the shack. "What is this place?"

"I dunno what it's called, but when people play on the beach, they come here to rinse the sand off their feet and then eat food," Franklin explained. "Lucy's brought me to a few different ones. Look!"

He trotted over to a patch of hard, gray ground in the middle of the grass. There was a small hole in the ground with a grate over it, and a long metal pipe that stuck out way, way high over Oliver's head. At the top, it curved over and pointed straight down again. Oliver could see from here that it was hollow.

"Stand under that," Franklin directed, pointing

to the pipe. Oliver moved over and stood in the center of the circle, glancing around uncertainly.

Franklin moved behind the pipe, and now Oliver could see a piece of metal sticking out of the ground next to it.

"Ready?" Franklin called. He bit down on the metal thing and wagged his tail.

Oliver blinked. "Ready for wha—"

The rest of his words were cut off when Franklin pulled the metal thing and a stream of freezing-cold water came pouring out of the pipe—right onto Oliver's head!

"Argh! Mugh! Phft!" Oliver sputtered. For maybe half a second, he felt a little indignant. Then he saw the icky black stuff running off his fur, streaming across the hard ground, and slipping down the hole with the grate. Oliver tilted his head back so that the water poured directly into his mouth. He swished and spit and spun around and around until he was completely drenched in fresh water.

It felt *great*.

"All done?" Franklin asked over the sound of the water rushing out of the pipe.

"Yeah!"

Franklin pulled the metal thing back to its starting position, and the stream of water slowed to a trickle. Oliver sighed happily, giving his back end a little wiggle to shake off the excess water.

"That was perfect," he said, beaming at Franklin. "Thanks!"

"No problem!" Franklin said. "It's called a shower. Lucy made me use one when I got muddy at the beach once. Her mom wouldn't let me in the car until they'd rinsed me off. I *hated* it. Not the mud. The water."

Oliver didn't know what a car was. And he couldn't imagine hating the feel of fresh, cold water rushing over you, washing away all the muck and grime.

But he was distracted by something else. Now that the black stuff was gone, along with its horrible smell, Oliver caught another scent. Something that made his stomach growl louder than ever.

"I smell clams!"

"Told ya!" Franklin gestured to the shack. "This is where people eat food that comes out of the water. There's probably tons of clams in there."

Oliver was beyond impressed that Franklin had smelled the clams from so far away. His ears might be enormous, but his nose was obviously his superpower!

"There's only one problem," Franklin added. "I don't know how to actually get inside."

"Hmm." Oliver looked around at the grass surrounding the shower. He spied a big, heavy rock and hurried over to examine it. "This is perfect!"

"But you don't have a clam yet!"

"I'm not gonna use it on a clam." Oliver faced the shack, a wide smile on his face. "I'm gonna use it to open *that*."

8

 LUCY

After two solid hours of scrubbing the slick black rocks, Lucy couldn't help but think the beach looked worse than ever.

The news reports they'd listened to in the car on the way to the lab had said the tanker had nearly reached the northern tip of Bainbridge Island, which was a few miles south of this beach.

"Shouldn't we go closer to the spill?" Lucy had asked Mom, who'd just followed an exit sign to Everett. "Won't they need more help there?"

"We'd only get in the way of the professionals," Mom replied. "They're probably going to have to do a shoreline flush, maybe even bring in the vacuum trucks. The best way for us to be helpful is to work on cleaning up an area that wasn't as hard-hit."

When she and Mom had first arrived at Marina Beach Park, Lucy privately thought the damage from the oil spill wasn't so bad. Sure, she could see patches of oil here and there, but most of the coastline was unharmed. But as the tide came in, it gradually undid all of Mom's and Lucy's hard scrubbing work.

"Another seagull over here!" Mom called, and Lucy leaped up. She made her way carefully over the oil-slick pebbles and toward Mom, who was crouched next to a quivering mound of black-and-gray feathers.

Mom's coworker Ellen hurried over with a medical kit. She knelt down next to the poor bird, her knees squelching in the muck. "Looks like a broken wing."

Lucy swallowed hard as Ellen pulled a splint from the kit. She wanted to cry for the poor seagull. It didn't make a sound as Ellen set its wing, just watched with what Lucy felt was a very stoic expression.

"The good news is, he should be pretty easy to clean up," Mom said, holding the seagull still as Ellen worked. "He managed not to get too covered."

So far, they'd rescued and cleaned off three seagulls and six crabs. The van from the lab was parked nearby, and it was stocked with enough supplies for basic medical care and cleaning. But any serious cases—animals with severe injuries or completely coated in oil—would have to be rushed back to the lab for proper care.

A sharp bark caused Lucy's head to snap to attention. She looked around hopefully, then her gaze fell on Rogue and she sighed. Lucy loved Ellen's pit bull, but right now the sight of the happy-go-lucky three-legged pup only made her miss Franklin even more.

"She probably found another crab," Ellen said, straightening up. "I'll take care of that if you're okay with the seagull, Sarah?"

"No problem," Mom replied. "We should probably take a lunch break soon."

Twenty minutes later, with the seagull cleaned

and resting in the van, Mom and Ellen took a cooler over to a nearby park bench. Ellen had brought sandwiches and apples, but Lucy felt too anxious to eat. She picked at her sandwich—tuna salad with pickles—while Mom and Ellen talked.

"Once we've done all we can here, we can head up to that little bay about a mile north," Mom suggested.

Lucy's stomach twisted. That was even farther from the farmer's market! This might be the only chance she got.

"Mom, is it okay if I go hang up the flyers I made for Franklin?" she asked, wrapping up the remains of her sandwich.

Mom looked startled. "Oh, sweetie—of course! I'm so sorry, with everything going on, I . . ." She paused, shaking her head. "Yes, go ahead. Be back in half an hour?"

"Thanks!" Lucy shot to her feet.

Ellen gave her a bracing, sympathetic smile. "I just know he's going to turn up, Lucy," she said.

Lucy tried to smile back. "Yeah."

She grabbed her backpack from the van and set off toward the farmer's market, walking as quickly as she could without actually running. On Mondays, the market didn't open until noon, so vendors were still setting up their booths. Lucy started by going from booth to booth, leaving a flyer with each vendor, before moving down to the pier.

The stench from the oil spill was getting stronger, and Lucy couldn't help wondering if anyone would even come to the farmer's market today. Maybe they would be curious about the spill. Or maybe this would keep people at home.

Which meant her chances of someone finding Franklin had gone down a *lot*.

Lucy tried not to think about that as she taped a flyer to a light pole on the boardwalk. Her gaze drifted down the pier, then to the beach . . . and the sight of a squirmy brown ball of fur caused her heart to soar.

But it wasn't Franklin. Even before she took a step forward, Lucy could tell the dog wasn't even a dachshund—it was too big. It was romping around with a golden retriever, and Lucy thought she could see a pug zipping around, too.

The dog park! She'd completely forgotten about it. Lucy jogged down the boardwalk, keeping her eyes on the frolicking dogs. If these people brought their dogs to this park every day, maybe one of them had spotted Franklin yesterday.

She entered the park, closing the gate carefully behind her. The pug sprinted up to her, leaping up and placing its paws on her knees, and Lucy giggled and gave it a pat on the head. She watched as the pug sprinted back over to its friends, then walked to where a few people sat on the benches with paper cups of coffee.

"Excuse me," Lucy said nervously, squeezing the stack of papers in her hand. The older woman with gray hair in a long braid down her back looked up first and smiled.

"Yes, dear?"

"I was wondering if any of you have seen this dog." Lucy held out the flyer.

The other two people, both young men probably a

few years older than Zach, glanced over curiously. A crease appeared in the woman's forehead as she took the flyer.

"Oh, goodness! What a cutie." She studied the photo carefully, then shook her head. "I can't say I've seen him, dear. I'm so sorry."

"Me, either," said the man in steel-rimmed glasses.

"What about yesterday?" Lucy asked. "That's when I . . . I lost him. It was around five o'clock, and we were on the pier . . ."

The man with the glasses nudged his partner. "Weren't you here with Oreo around then?"

"Yeah, that's right," the man said, giving the flyer another look. Then he shook his head. "I'm really sorry but I don't think I saw him."

"That's okay." Lucy swallowed back a lump in her throat.

"We'll keep an eye out for you, dear!" the woman called as she headed back to the gate. Lucy heard her murmur to the men, "That poor thing." She wondered if the woman meant her or Franklin.

After taping a flyer to the gate, Lucy turned to head back to Mom and the van . . . but then a group of people in matching aqua-blue polo shirts caught her eye. They were down on the beach, and two of them held large, expensive-looking cameras. Patches of oil had begun to appear on the shore, and the rest of the group were spreading out and beginning to clean while the other two filmed.

A familiar laugh reached Lucy's ears, and her breath caught in her throat. She took a step forward, her eyes scanning the polo shirt crew until she spotted a boy with auburn hair and ruddy, wind-burned cheeks.

"Zach!"

Her brother's head jerked up, and his eyes widened. "Luce?"

"Hi!" Lucy cried, scrambling down the grassy, sandy hill to get to the beach. Zach jogged over, sweeping her up in a hug.

"Aw, it's so good to see you!" he exclaimed after setting her down. "What are you doing here?"

His brown eyes scanned the parking lot by the dog park, and Lucy knew he was looking for Mom's car. "I'm looking for Franklin."

Zach's smile faded. "What?"

"We brought him to the farmer's market yesterday, and he got off his leash." Lucy said it as flatly as possible. The last thing she wanted was to end up sobbing on the beach in front of her big brother and his friends. "I just was putting up flyers."

"Man, Luce. That's the *worst*. I'm so sorry." Zach held out his hand. "Give me a few, okay? I'll pass them around."

"Thanks," Lucy said gratefully, handing over what was left of her stack. "So are you guys here to help with the cleanup?"

"Yeah. Awful, isn't it?" Zach sighed, glancing out at the tanker in the distance. "We had to cancel all tours for the day. Probably for the rest of the week, maybe even next week, too."

"I'm sorry." Lucy paused. "What about . . . Does this mean ABZ Tours is . . . closing?"

Zach looked amused. "Worried about me going out of business already, eh?"

"No!" Lucy said, flustered. "I don't—I never—I just mean you can't make money because of the oil spill!"

"We'll be all right for a month or so." Zach motioned for her to walk with him, and they headed toward the group. "We just landed a huge sponsor last week. Bryson talked to them this morning—they're going to help us organize a campaign to raise money for the cleanup, and they're donating a skimmer we can use to help."

"What's a skimmer?"

"It's this special device we can attach to the back of our boat that kind of traps the oil," Zach explained. "They're sending someone to deliver it this afternoon, and I'm going to take the boat out. Alex is talking about it on the livestream right now, I think."

He pointed, and Lucy saw his friend Alex, a tall, reed-thin boy with dark brown skin and a scruffy beard, standing near the water. He was holding his phone out to capture the tanker and talking in a low voice.

"Is this for your YouTube channel?" Lucy asked. Zach had sent her the link to their channel back in June. She'd been their very first subscriber—even before they had uploaded a video.

"Yeah. Lots of our subs are local, so we're hoping to help get the word out so that more people will come help." Zach's expression brightened, and he turned to Lucy. "Hey, want to say something about Franklin?"

Lucy's mouth opened and closed. "Um, I . . ." She knew she should say yes, but the idea of actually being on a livestream while who knew how many people were watching made her kind of nervous. Besides, what would Mom say if she found out?

"Tell you what," Zach said, rescuing her. "Text me a video of him, and I'll share it. Okay?"

"Thanks, Zach." Lucy felt intensely relieved. She pulled her phone out, but a sudden shout nearly caused her to drop it.

"Guys! Come quick!"

Zach turned sharply, and Lucy saw Bryson farther down the beach. He was crouching next to what Lucy thought at first was a log. Then her eyes registered the curve of its back, the tail . . .

"Oh no," she breathed.

Zach was already running toward Bryson, the others not far behind him. Lucy stood there numbly. It was too big to be Franklin, but it was definitely an animal.

Steeling herself, Lucy walked to where the group had gathered around the creature. It was completely covered in oil, but Lucy could make out four paws. Moving around to stand next to Zach, she saw the creature's face just as it opened its eyes. It gazed up at them, looking disoriented and more than a little frightened. The tail flickered a bit, but otherwise, it didn't move.

"An otter," Bryson said softly. "Poor thing."

"What should we do?" Zach asked. "Take it to a vet?"

"I don't think we should move it," a girl next to Alex said. "What if something's broken, and we make it worse?"

"I'll go get some towels from the car," Alex said, turning and jogging toward the parking lot.

As the others continued to talk in hushed tones, Lucy took a few steps back. Opening the messages app on her phone, she sent a quick text.

The moment she sent the text, Lucy's hands started to sweat. She hung back as her brother and his friends discussed what to do. Alex returned with a pile of towels, and he and Zach began to wipe as much of the oil as they could off the otter without moving it. Lucy's heart ached for the poor otter. Other than the occasional twitch of its tail, it barely moved at all.

When the van pulled into the parking lot, Lucy was the first one to notice.

"Zach, I, um . . ."

But Zach was talking to Bryson, and he didn't hear her. Lucy's gaze moved from him to Mom, who was hurrying down the grassy hill carrying the medical kit. Ellen was at her side, holding a small stretcher. Back in the van, Lucy could see Rogue's soulful brown eyes in the window of the passenger seat.

Mom waved when she saw Lucy. "Hey, hon! So glad you . . ."

She trailed off, her eyes moving to the group gathered around the otter.

Lucy gulped, stepping to the side and looking at Zach. He glanced up at Mom and Ellen, then did a double take.

"Zach?"

"Mom?"

They stared at each other in shock. Ellen's mouth was a round O of surprise, and Zach's friends fell quiet.

"Oh, hey, Ms. Carmichael!" Alex said a little too brightly.

Mom blinked. Then she raised an eyebrow at Lucy.

"There's the otter," Lucy blurted out, pointing.

"Oh, gosh, look at this poor thing . . ." Ellen hurried over to the otter. Mom shot Lucy one last look that was something between frustration and sadness, then went to join Ellen.

Folding his arms across his chest, Zach stepped away and stood next to Lucy. "You texted her," he murmured. It wasn't a question.

Lucy winced. "I had to. It was an emergency."

A moment later, Mom stood up and looked around. "We need to get this otter to the lab as fast as possible," she said briskly. Lucy couldn't help noticing she avoided Zach's eyes as she spoke. "Can I get two of you to help me and Ellen get her onto a stretcher, please?"

Zach and Alex obliged immediately, and the others watched as the four of them slowly, carefully lifted the otter onto the stretcher. Mom and Ellen lifted the stretcher and began carrying it to the van.

"Let's go, Lucy," Mom called. There wasn't even a trace of anger in her voice, but Lucy flinched anyway. She caught Zach rolling his eyes, and her stomach clenched with the same old anxiety.

"Um, I'll text you," she told him. "Let you know how she's doing. The otter, I mean."

"'Kay." Zach gave her a half smile. "Send me that video of Franklin, too. I'm gonna help you find him, Luce. Don't worry."

Lucy nodded, then turned away before he could see the tears in her eyes and hurried after Mom.

9

 **FRANKLIN**

Franklin was fascinated by the way Oliver used the rock. To Franklin, rocks were just rocks. They weren't great for chewing—nothing like a good stick—and they didn't smell particularly interesting.

But Oliver had called the rock a "tool." Franklin knew about tools. Sarah had a big black box full of them in the garage. When Franklin was still very, *very* young, he'd thought the box was filled with shiny silver puppy toys. He'd sprinted around the garage in circles with something called a screwdriver in his mouth while Sarah chased him and Lucy giggled uncontrollably.

But Sarah could fix things with tools. And the way she held them and worked with them looked an awful lot like Oliver right now.

The otter stood in front of the door to the shack. He was tapping and knocking the rock against the door in a complicated rhythm, and from the way his head was cocked, it seemed as though he was listening for something. But the door remained shut. After a few minutes, Franklin spoke up.

"See that silver thing over your head?" he said, and Oliver glanced up. "That's a doorknob. That's what people use to open doors."

"Hmm." Oliver studied the knob. Then he jumped and swiped the rock at the knob. When nothing happened, he tried it a few more times, then sighed.

"Is there any other way people get in and out of places?"

Franklin considered this. He gazed at the shack, and then he perked up.

"The window!" He hurried over, gesturing for Oliver to follow him. "Those open, too. Sarah opens the living room windows sometimes. Once I jumped out and ran around the backyard until I got dizzy. It was so fun!" Franklin paused, remembering. "Although I think Lucy was kind of scared."

Oliver scrambled up the drainpipe and stood on the ledge. Franklin watched as the otter gently tapped the rock against the window. *Tap tap tap.* Then a little more insistently. *TAP TAP TAP.* And then:

CRASH!

Franklin let out a bark of surprise and leaped back as the window shattered. Oliver ducked and covered his face as shards of glass flew everywhere.

"What happened?"

"You broke it," Franklin said. "That's not how humans open windows. But it worked!"

Oliver lowered his arms and faced the inside of the shack. He took in a long, deep breath.

"Clams!"

"Wait for me!" Franklin exclaimed as Oliver jumped through the window.

Spotting an overturned bucket, Franklin hurried

over and hopped on. From there, it was a pretty easy jump to the window ledge, even with his admittedly short legs.

Inside, he spotted Oliver standing in front of a giant metal door, rapping and tapping with his rock. Franklin glanced around. This room looked kind of like the kitchen at home, only way bigger and with a lot more pots and pans on the shelves.

"Oh, wait!" Oliver said suddenly. "The doorknob!"

Franklin turned, expecting to see Oliver pulling on the latch to the metal door. Instead, he saw the otter rearing back with his rock, and then—*SMASH!*

The latch broke off, falling to the linoleum floor with a clatter. The door popped open, and Oliver cheered.

Franklin joined him, and they pushed the door all the way open together. A blast of chilly air greeted them, along with . . .

"Wow." Oliver's eyes were huge. "I've never seen this many clams in one place in my whole life!"

There were bags and bags of not just clams, but

also crabs, their legs poking through the netting. Franklin could smell fish as well, although those were higher up on the shelves. But Oliver clearly only cared about the clams.

He used the rock to slice the netting of one bag open, laughing with delight as the pearly gray clams spilled out across the floor. Not wasting a moment, Oliver sat down and set to work with his rock. First he smashed the shell, then he popped the clam in his mouth, then he tossed the empty shell to the side. All of that took him about one second.

Franklin was greatly impressed. He could snarf down a bowl of chow in a minute flat. Sarah often chided him for eating too quickly.

But Oliver ate even faster than Franklin!

Thinking about his morning bowl of chow made Franklin's tummy growl. Oliver must have heard, because he smashed open five clams in a row—*smash smash smash smash smash*—and pushed them over to Franklin.

"Thanks!" Franklin said, but he hesitated. He'd

never had clams before. Cautiously, he leaned down and took a few discerning sniffs. Then he picked a clam out of its shell, held it between his teeth for a moment, and swallowed.

It was delicious!

For a while, they ate in silence. Well, Franklin thought as he gulped down another clam, not *silence*. They didn't talk, but between the smashing and the slurping, they were making quite a bit of noise.

Franklin ate until he was full, then sat back on his haunches and groomed while Oliver continued to eat. And eat. And *eat*.

"Wow," Franklin said at last. "Look at that pile of shells!"

Oliver popped another clam into his mouth and chucked the shell into the pile behind him. It was almost as tall as Franklin! Which, Franklin had to admit, wasn't all *that* tall, but it was still a whole lot of clams for one baby otter to eat.

Finally, Oliver let out a sigh of contentment and rubbed his belly. "I feel so much better now."

"Me, too," Franklin said. "What should we do now?"

Oliver's expression changed, his whiskers drooping. "Well, I . . . I want to go home. I want to find my momma. But I can't just hop back in the ocean. Not with that black goo everywhere."

Franklin's ears pricked up at the word *ocean*. It took his brain a few seconds to catch up with his instincts. When it did, his tail went *thump thump thump* on the tile floor.

"I bet Sarah can help you!"

"Who?"

"Lucy's mom!" Franklin was on all fours now. "She's a . . . um . . ." He struggled to remember the word Lucy used when she told people what her mom did for work. "She's an ocean . . . person!"

That *definitely* was not what Lucy called her.

Oliver looked perplexed. "People don't live in the ocean."

"She doesn't live in it. But she knows everything about it."

"How can someone know everything about some-place if they don't live there?"

Franklin opened his mouth, then closed it. It was a fair point, he had to admit.

"I'm just saying, she knows a whole lot about the ocean and especially all the animals that live in it and I bet you anything she knows what that black goo is, too," he informed Oliver. "Sarah can definitely help you find your momma and get you both back home!"

"Okay." Oliver sat up and smiled. "So where is she?"

Once again, Franklin wavered. He never had to worry about finding Lucy or her mom. They always found *him*. But it was becoming pretty clear to Franklin that this wasn't their usual game of hide-and-seek. He'd never been away from Lucy for this long. If she knew where to find him, she would've done it by now. Franklin was certain of that.

"Your nose!" Oliver exclaimed suddenly.

Franklin swatted his nose with his paw. "Did I get clam on it?"

"No!" Oliver laughed. "I mean your sense of smell.

It's amazing! You smelled these clams all the way from the beach. You just need to smell your way home!"

"That's the problem," Franklin told him. "I think I'm too far away from home. I can't smell Lucy or Sarah at all."

Not for the first time since fleeing the farmer's market, Franklin felt worried. What if he never found his way back? What if he never saw Lucy again?

Oliver gave him a sympathetic smile. "Well, what if we go back the way you came from? If we go far enough, I bet you'll be able to pick up the scent eventually. Do you remember how you got here?"

Franklin tried to think. He remembered running into the woods, and he remembered finding the bay. But everything in between was just a squirrelly haze. His tail flopped to the floor.

"It's okay," Oliver said comfortingly. "Maybe if we go outside and look around, you'll remember!"

"Why not?" Feeling slightly cheerier, Franklin trotted over to the broken window, Oliver right on his heels.

Once they were outside, Franklin took a good look around. He knew the gravelly path they'd come up would lead back to the bay. And he could hear the not-too-distant roar of cars coming from the opposite direction, which meant a busy road was close—that *definitely* wasn't the right way. There was nothing but trees on either side.

Franklin remembered emerging from the woods onto the bay . . . and the water was on his right. Which meant . . .

"This way!"

He set off confidently into the woods, tail high and nose alert. Oliver scrambled to keep up.

They found a nice dirt path right away. Franklin couldn't be sure it was the same path he'd wandered down yesterday. But he couldn't be certain it wasn't, either.

The woods smelled bright and fresh and mossy. *Much* better than the chemical stink of the black stuff all over the beach. Franklin trotted at a brisk pace, Oliver at his side, and for a while they traveled in silence. Franklin assumed the otter was enjoying the walk as much as he was—after all, who didn't love a good walk? But when he glanced at Oliver and saw his miserable expression, Franklin stopped in his tracks.

"What's wrong?"

"Nothing!" Oliver said a little too quickly. Then he sighed. "It's just . . . my friend Lulu said playing on land was really fun. I've always wanted to do this. But swimming is so much better!"

Franklin suppressed a shudder. He liked Oliver, but he would *never* understand how anyone could love anything as awful as *swimming*.

He was about to respond when a scent caught his attention. Franklin lifted his head and took a good, long sniff. It was a scent he recognized, a mix of cherries and coffee and the general odor of humans.

The farmer's market!

Eagerly, Franklin turned to tell Oliver that they really were on the right track. But then the tiniest movement caught his eye, and he froze.

Several feet behind Oliver, nestled between two bushes, was a familiar furry brown creature.

It went stock-still, beady black eyes locking on to Franklin's. A tiny part of Franklin's brain yelled, *No! Don't do it! Stay on the path to the farmer's market!* But a much, much *bigger* part of Franklin's brain was only focused on one thing.

"SQUIRREL!"

"Wha—" Alarmed, Oliver leaped out of the way as Franklin charged at the squirrel. It darted between the bushes, and Franklin didn't hesitate—he plowed through them and tore across the grass as fast as his legs would carry him.

The world became a blur of green, the center of focus a fluffy brown tail. Franklin let out a happy bark as he darted around a tree and leaped over a fallen log. He still had that tail in his sights! No way would the squirrel get away this time! It kept trying to shake Franklin, zipping off to the left, dodging right, changing directions every other second. But Franklin kept up with every turn.

Until the squirrel scrambled up a tree.

Franklin jumped up, placing his front paws on the trunk. "Hey, that's cheating!" he cried, but he wasn't really mad about it. Through the leafy branches, he could just make out the squirrel jumping to another tree, then another, until it was out of sight.

Only then did Franklin remember Oliver.

Slightly panicked, he turned around just as Oliver stumbled through a cluster of bushes, panting.

"What?" Oliver gasped, rubbing his side. "Why?"

"Squirrel," Franklin said matter-of-factly. "Sorry. I can't control myself."

Oliver looked completely bewildered. Then his expression changed, and his eyes went wide. "Wait. Do you hear that?"

All Franklin could hear was the pounding of his own heart. But his ears perked up, and after a moment, he heard it, too. A trickly, burbly sound.

"Water!"

This time, it was Oliver who sprinted off and Franklin who had to rush to catch up. He followed the otter through the woods, listening as the sound grew louder and louder. Finally, they reached a stream—and to Franklin's relief, the water was nice and clear.

"No black goo!" Oliver cheered before leaping into the stream with a *splash!* Franklin laughed as the otter flipped onto his back and floated there, faceup, a big grin on his face. He hurried to the edge of the stream and drank deeply. After all those clams, not to mention the epic squirrel chase, Franklin was extremely thirsty.

Once he was finished, he looked up to see Oliver waiting with an expectant look on his face.

"What?" Franklin asked.

"Well, come on!"

"In the water?" Franklin snorted. "No chance."

"But this is our new path!"

"Huh?"

Oliver gestured at the stream. "You said the place you left Lucy was by the water. Water leads to water! It's all connected."

Franklin considered this.

"Okay, but I'm not getting in. I'll just walk along the side."

"You're missing out!" Oliver teased. Then without warning, he slapped his tail down on the water.

Splash!

"Hey!" Franklin sputtered, but Oliver was already swimming down the stream, laughing as Franklin shook himself to get the water off his fur. "I'll get you for that!"

He took off running, although of course he had no intention of getting in the stream. But it was fun to dodge the splashes that Oliver kept sending his way. He also spotted a few more nice-looking rocks and scooped them up in his mouth to give to Oliver later. He could tell the otter wasn't too fond of the first one Franklin had found. Maybe one of these would be better.

A tiny part of Franklin's brain, the part that told him not to chase squirrels, was trying to tell him something else now. Something about how it was pretty sure they were going in the opposite direction they'd been heading before. Which meant they were getting farther and farther away from the farmer's market, and Lucy.

But Oliver said that water led to water. And who was Franklin to argue about water with an otter?

10

 **OLIVER**

Oliver was thrilled to be in fresh, clean water again. Although it was really different from the seawater he was used to. It was a little bit harder to float, and the taste was almost sweet—not the salty tang he knew so well. But it was water, and he felt more at home.

He could tell Franklin wasn't quite as thrilled as he was about their new path. But Oliver was completely positive that this would lead them to the farmer's market.

"All the water you'll find on land is connected to the ocean," Lulu's mother had told her and Oliver once. "There are little streams of water, and brooks, and lakes, and there are rivers, too!"

Oliver had been fascinated. So had Lulu. One thing Lulu hadn't done yet was swim in a river. But her family had, and one day she would, too.

"Some rivers are so wide," Lulu had told Oliver eagerly, "you can be on one side and not even see the land on the other side!"

"Wow!" Oliver had exclaimed.

"And there are river otters!" Lulu went on. "They live there, just like we live in the sea."

That had been hard for Oliver to imagine. After all, why would any otter want to live anywhere but the sea if they had the choice? But now, floating on his back under the shade of the trees, Oliver thought being a river otter might not be such a bad thing after all.

Not that this was a river. It was a stream. He wondered if stream otters existed, and decided they probably didn't.

"Oliver!" Franklin called suddenly. His voice was

distant, and Oliver sat up with a splash. He'd been so lost in thought he hadn't realized how far he'd drifted from Franklin.

"Sorry!" he called, stretching out an arm and grabbing a low-hanging branch. He clung to it as Franklin struggled to climb over a large rock that took up most of the shore. Oliver could see his furry face pop up over the rock, then vanish as he slid back down, over and over.

Frowning, Oliver glanced up the shore. It was getting rockier and rockier, plus there were tons of gnarled roots and thick clusters of bushes. Pretty soon, it was going to be impossible for Franklin to walk along the shore at all.

"Franklin, I think . . . Franklin?!" Oliver looked around frantically. He couldn't hear the dachshund's pants and the scrabble of his paws on the rock anymore. "Franklin! Where'd you go?"

"Right here!" Franklin emerged from the bushes, and Oliver relaxed. "That rock was too big. But good news! There's a trail that runs along the stream."

"Oh." Oliver felt slightly deflated. "Or . . . you could swim in the stream."

Franklin wrinkled his nose. "I'm not a good swimmer."

"Right."

Slowly and with great reluctance, Oliver began to make his way to the shore. It wasn't just that he preferred the water. It was that this way would be so much faster.

Plus—and he would never say this to Franklin— there were no squirrels in the stream. What if they were walking along the trail and Franklin took off after another squirrel? Oliver had barely been able to keep up with him. They could be separated! And Oliver didn't much like the idea of going on this adventure alone.

Oliver reached the shore and shook himself off. Then he spotted a long, thin branch on the pebbles and inspiration struck.

"We can make a raft!"

Franklin tilted his head. "What's a raft?"

Oliver was already gathering sticks. "It's some-thing we otters use when we want to float together. It's kind of like a boat! We use seaweed, but I bet sticks will work—especially these really bendy ones, not ones that snap in half easily. Can you help me?"

Franklin's tail began to wag furiously. "Help you get sticks? That's my favorite game!"

And he took off, slip-sliding over the wet rocks. Oliver felt a lot more cheerful as he added another stick to his quickly growing pile. Momma had taught him how to weave a really good raft. The last one he'd made had been big enough to hold him, Lulu, Pearl, and Sammy.

Oliver grinned at the memory. The four of them had floated so far out on the sea, they couldn't see land in any direction! Best of all, they'd seen a whale breach the surface of the water. Oliver had looked the whale right in the eye just before it sank back beneath the waves.

And then Momma had swum out to get them.

"You can't go out this far yet, Ollie!" she chided, tugging the raft back toward home. "What if you got lost?"

Lulu and the others had stifled their giggles, and Oliver's face burned with shame. At the time, he'd been so frustrated with Momma. She never let him have any fun!

Now, though, he knew she was right. He'd strayed too far from home, and look where he was now: floating on a stream with a dog!

But the stream would take him to the ocean, Oliver told himself now, beginning to weave the sticks together. It had to. Lulu's momma was never wrong about this stuff.

"Ith thith enuth?"

Startled, Oliver looked up to see Franklin standing in front of him. His tail was wagging furiously, and in his mouth was an enormous bundle of sticks.

"Wow!" Oliver exclaimed. "These are perfect."

Franklin dropped the sticks, looking extremely

proud of himself. Then he spat out three rocks. "I got you these, too!"

Oliver stared at the rocks. "For me?"

"Yeah! Since you lost yours."

"Thanks!" Oliver tentatively picked up the rocks one by one. They were all wrong, all three of them. But he didn't want to hurt Franklin's feelings, so he tucked them in his pocket.

Franklin looked pleased. "Are these enough sticks for a boat, though?"

"It's enough for a raft for two," Oliver said, busying himself with the sticks. "It's not exactly a boat. It's flat and we'll still be a little bit in the water. But you won't have to swim!"

When the dachshund didn't answer, Oliver glanced up. Franklin's tail was drooping.

"I'll get wet?"

"Just a little." Oliver felt bad. "But on the bright side, we'll get there faster *and* we can rest at the same time!"

"I guess that doesn't sound too bad," Franklin admitted.

Oliver finished the raft and stepped back to admire it. Franklin eyed the raft doubtfully.

"You sure that's going to float with both of us on it?"

"Yup!" Oliver pushed the raft out onto the water and held it steady. "Come on, try it!"

Franklin stuck a paw daintily into the water and grimaced. But he made his way to the raft and climbed on . . . then stood there, four legs stiff as a board, his posture so rigid that Oliver couldn't help giggling.

"You're not going to stand like that the whole way, are you?"

"Um . . ."

"You'll lose your balance once I get on and we start moving," Oliver pointed out. "Then you'll fall into the stream and get *super* wet."

That seemed to convince Franklin. Slowly and stiffly, he lay down on the raft. Carefully, Oliver climbed on, and they set off down the stream.

After a few seconds, Franklin relaxed slightly. "This isn't so bad!" he said.

Oliver beamed. "I know, right?"

"I can't wait to see Lucy again," Franklin said, his tail thumping against the raft. "She's going to be so happy to see me."

Oliver smiled but said nothing. He was wondering if Lucy's mom, Sarah, would really be able to help him find his own momma. The more he thought about it, the more doubtful he felt. Even if this Sarah was an expert on ocean animals, how would she know where to find Momma? And what about all that black stuff . . . What if it had spread from Puget Sound through the strait?

What if he didn't even *have* a home anymore?

Oliver tried to shake these thoughts off. It was starting to get warm now that the sun was higher in the sky, and before long, Oliver began to feel drowsy. He had a belly full of clams, and the sun felt so good on his fur, and the water was so gentle and cool beneath them . . .

He heard Franklin let out a little snore and realized he'd fallen asleep. His paws were twitching, and

Oliver wondered if he was dreaming about chasing that squirrel.

Oliver yawned widely. A nap sounded pretty good, actually. His eyelids drooped, then closed. *The current is really picking up speed,* he thought. *I'll be home soon.*

Then he drifted off to sleep.

LUCY

Sound Marine Lab was one of Lucy's favorite places. It was a small lab, nothing at all like the larger marine biology lab at the university. They had a staff of six, and Mom and Ellen had been there longer than anyone.

The inside of the lab seemed clinical and sterile at first, but there was actually so much life inside! When Lucy had been little, she'd spent hours staring in fascination at all the aquariums and tubs filled with fish, seahorses, hermit crabs, and other kinds of marine life. Sometimes Mom would even let her peer through a microscope at algae or other interesting things.

The lab was so clean and organized, it always made Lucy feel calm. But she wasn't so sure that would be the case today.

The van ride from the beach to the lab had been tense. Sarah and Ellen were unusually quiet, and Lucy tried to tell herself that it was only because they were worried about the otter. The poor thing was strapped onto its stretcher, and Lucy could barely tear her eyes off it as Mom pulled out of the parking lot.

But Zach was following the van in his car, a bright blue VW Bug. And Lucy saw the way Mom's eyes kept glancing in the rearview mirror. Her expression was difficult to read.

Lucy's stomach was doing flip-flops as they parked and hopped out of the van. Suddenly, the urge to cuddle Franklin was almost overwhelming. Her puppy had comforted her all those months when it seemed like Mom and Zach had argued every day. She swallowed back her tears and closed the van door while Mom and Ellen carefully and quickly slid the stretcher carrying the otter out of the back.

They headed straight for the lab, but Lucy lingered behind while Zach parked. His eyes were on Mom's back as she disappeared inside the lab, then he turned to Lucy.

"Haven't been here in a while."

"Yeah." Lucy tried to smile at him, but she hated the uncertain expression on his face. "Thanks for coming."

"Of course, Luce." Zach slung his arm around her, and they walked into the lab together.

Inside was all white floors and walls and glass containers and shiny science equipment. Mom and Ellen were already pulling on their lab coats and gloves. Lucy and Zach hung back and watched in silence as Ellen began filling a plastic tub with water while Mom prepared IV bags filled with fluid. At last, Mom cleared her throat.

"What time exactly did you find her?"

Her. Lucy gazed at the poor otter, all slick with oil.

"Um . . ." Zach sounded hesitant. "Bryson found her, I guess it was about twenty minutes ago or so?"

Lucy pulled out her phone and checked her text to Mom. "It was quarter after one," she said. "I texted you right away."

Mom nodded. "And how long had you been at that part of the beach?"

"Maybe ten minutes or so?" Lucy replied, confused.

There was a pause, and Mom sighed. "Not you."

"Oh." Lucy glanced nervously at Zach. His lips had tightened into a thin line.

"Half an hour. We started at the dog park and were making our way north."

"Anyone else doing cleanup on that beach?"

"Not that I saw."

Mom nodded curtly. Throughout the entire brief conversation, she kept her eyes on the bags, not glancing at Zach even once.

"Why does that matter?" Lucy couldn't help asking.

"The spill happened last night," Ellen explained. "There are no otter habitats near that beach, or else you no doubt would have found more of them. We're trying to figure out how far this little lady came." She stroked the otter's head gently as she spoke. "Based on her condition, she likely got caught up in the oil spill as it was happening."

Lucy was thunderstruck. "You mean she'd been lying there on the beach like that all night?"

Mom's expression softened. "I know it's awful, but we're going to do everything we can for her. You did the right thing, texting me right away. She's getting the help she needs thanks to you."

Her gaze shifted to Zach, who stiffened. For a moment, the two of them just looked at each other.

"And you," Mom said finally. "It's good you and your friends were out there helping with the cleanup."

Lucy held her breath as Zach shrugged. "It's part of the job," he replied, putting a tiny bit of emphasis on the word *job*.

"They've got a sponsor!" Lucy burst out, and Mom raised her eyebrows. "They're going to do a campaign to raise money for cleaning up the oil spill. And they're getting a skimmer."

As soon as she said it, she regretted having spoken at all. Lucy had thought for a brief moment that maybe Mom would be as impressed as she was by the success of ABZ Tours. But instead, a look of annoyance flashed across Mom's face.

"That's nice," was all she said, and then her attention was back on the otter.

As Mom and Ellen began carefully wiping the thicker patches of oil off the otter's fur, Zach turned to Lucy. "I'm gonna take off, if that's okay," he said under his breath. "The skimmer's probably been delivered by now, and I want to get it out on the water."

Lucy swallowed and nodded, trying not to look too disappointed. "Yeah, okay. Thanks for coming."

"Keep me posted on the otter, okay?"

"I will."

Zach gave her a quick, one-armed hug, then set off with his hands stuffed in his pockets. He didn't look at Mom, and she only glanced up after he was gone.

"Ready?" Ellen asked, with a touch of forced cheer in her voice. Mom nodded, and Lucy moved closer to watch as they gently lifted the otter from the stretcher and laid her in the shallow bath. The water instantly blackened, and Lucy felt tears prick her eyes as the otter gazed up at her dolefully.

"Why isn't she moving more?" she whispered.

"She's in early stages of hypothermia," Ellen explained, using a cloth to clean the otter's paws. "The oil matted her fur so much that it stopped protecting her from the cold."

"It's not that cold outside, though!"

"But it is in deeper waters," Mom said. "She must have been swimming when she got caught up in the spill. Oh, hang on . . ."

Lucy and Ellen watched as Mom carefully felt beneath the otter's arm. Her face lit up with a smile as she pulled out a rock.

"My goodness!" Ellen exclaimed. "All that she went through, and she didn't lose her rock. That's impressive!"

Lucy was bewildered. "Her rock?"

"Otters use rocks as tools to open clams and crabs," Mom explained. "They choose one rock when they're very young, and they keep it their whole life."

"That's so cute!" Lucy exclaimed, delighted.

"You didn't tell her the best part, Sarah," Ellen added, grinning at Lucy. "They have a pocket for it!"

"A pocket?" Lucy moved closer as Mom gently lifted the otter's arm. Sure enough, there was a little pocket in the otter's fur!

"Lucy, how 'bout you clean her rock while we finish her bath?" Ellen suggested.

"Great idea!" Mom held the rock out to Lucy. But Lucy's eyes were still on the otter's pocket.

"It kind of looks like there's something else in there," she said, pointing to the tiny bulge in the otter's underarm.

Mom and Ellen looked, too. "Maybe some debris got stuck in the pocket?" Mom mused, carefully slipping her fingers inside again. Ellen caressed the otter's head gently, but she didn't seem bothered. Lucy wondered if maybe she was still too cold to feel them touching her.

"Well, look at that." Mom held out another rock, her brows knit.

"She has two!" Lucy said, smiling. "Maybe that's her backup rock."

"I've never seen that before," Ellen said, her expression perplexed. "What odd behavior."

Mom handed Lucy both rocks, and she took them over to the sink and carefully washed them off. Behind her, Mom and Ellen set to work rinsing the otter, constantly draining the oily water and refilling the tub.

Lucy set the rocks on the stainless steel counter and gazed at them. One was large and sturdy and heavy. The other was smaller, and wider on one side than the other. Two special rocks. But Mom and Ellen said otters only had one special lifelong rock.

Maybe this otter was carrying another otter's rock? Did otters do that?

Lucy was about to ask Mom when her phone buzzed. She pulled it out and saw a text from Zach.

ZC: Send me that vid of Franklin!

Lucy's eyes widened, and she quickly opened her camera app. In all the fuss over finding the otter, she'd completely forgotten about Zach's promise to help her find her puppy.

She scrolled through her most recent videos, her heart thumping painfully when she landed on one of Franklin. She'd taken it when they'd had lunch at the farmer's market. Franklin was sitting up straight, his posture perfect, on top of the picnic table. Lucy had put him there so she'd have a background of the water and the mountains. Franklin's eyes were fixed on a point just above the camera, his tongue lolling. Lucy had had to hold a treat high in the air to get him to sit still long enough to take a few seconds of video. In the last second, Franklin lunged for the treat and Lucy shrieked with laughter.

Her throat tightened as she sent the video to Zach. His response was immediate.

ZC: *Such a cute little guy!*
ZC: *We're gonna blast this out everywhere, okay? Tons of people will be coming out to help with cleanup. Someone will spot him sooner or later!*

Lucy's spirits lifted. She texted back several heart emojis, then pocketed her phone. When she looked up, her eyes briefly met Mom's.

Mom glanced away, but Lucy knew she'd seen her texting. "How's the otter?" she asked tentatively.

"We'll start doing some tests when she's all clean," Mom said, gently sponging the otter's paws. She smiled at Lucy. "But her temperature's already up, so that's a great sign."

"Good." Lucy's shoulders sagged with relief.

As she watched Mom and Ellen work, she couldn't help picturing Zach and his friends on the beach right now, combing through the muck to look for more animals that needed help. Before Mom had arrived in the van, Lucy had allowed herself to feel the tiniest shred of hope that once her mother and brother saw each other, everything would go back to normal. That they would laugh and hug and Mom would see how cool Zach's business was and Zach would see that Mom only wanted what was best for him and all would be forgiven.

But things were as tense as ever. Maybe her family would never go back to normal again.

12

 **FRANKLIN**

Franklin flew through the trees. Literally. He had wings! He could see the squirrel up ahead, its eyes widening as it glanced back and saw Franklin swooping down.

At last, he was going to catch the squirrel!

But a huge gust of wind came along and nearly blew Franklin into a tree. His muscles tensed as he fought to stay on course. The wind grew stronger and stronger, and now Franklin could feel his claws come out, and someone was shouting—was it the squirrel?

"Franklin?"

No. Was it Lucy?

"Franklin!"

No. But he did recognize the voice . . .

"Franklin, wake up!"

Wake up? Franklin blinked, and the trees around him began to blur. His wings vanished, and he plummeted to the forest floor.

"Arf!" Franklin's head jerked up, and water sprayed his face. "W-what?" he sputtered, shaking his head. His claws were digging into the ground—no, the raft. The raft Oliver had built so they could float down the stream.

Only they weren't floating anymore. They were *flying.*

"What is that?" Oliver cried, staring straight ahead. He'd dug his claws into the raft just like Franklin. "Is that the ocean?"

Franklin squinted. They were speeding down the stream, which was much, much wider than it had been when he'd drifted off to sleep. Up ahead, he saw what Oliver was talking about—a line of gray that did look kind of like the ocean on the horizon. But it wasn't the ocean. Franklin could tell by the slightly sweet smell, which wasn't at all like the salty tang of ocean air. They sped closer and closer and Franklin's eyes adjusted and suddenly he realized he'd been looking at it all wrong, the line, because it wasn't a line.

It was a *drop*.

"We need to get off this stream!" Franklin cried. But even as he said it, he knew it was impossible. Land on either side of them was way too far for Franklin to swim. And with the current moving this fast, even Oliver probably wouldn't make it.

"Just hold on tight to the raft!" Oliver called back. The otter didn't sound frightened at all, Franklin thought, trying to find some comfort in that. But then again, Oliver would be just fine if he fell into the water. Otters lived in the water, after all.

Dachshunds most certainly did not.

There was nothing to do but hold on for dear life and watch as that line grew closer and closer and closer, and then . . .

"WHOAAAAAAAA!"

Franklin heard Oliver's shout as their raft fell, and he would have laughed if he hadn't felt so panicked. The steep drop lasted for three terrifying seconds, and then the raft slapped onto the water, sending a wave splashing over the two animals.

Oliver was laughing, and Franklin had to admit that it was sort of fun, except for the water part.

"I think this is a river!" Oliver managed to say as their raft picked up speed once more. Franklin didn't respond. His teeth were firmly clamped down on the raft, because the current was rough here and he was *not* going to fall into the water.

Great big rocks stuck up out of the river, which twisted and turned and dipped. The raft bumped against one of the rocks and spun around and around while still flying forward, making Franklin feel dizzy. How were they ever going to get off this thing and back to land?

"Mountains!" Oliver shouted suddenly. Franklin did his best to look up with his teeth still gripping the raft. He was startled to realize that the mountains that he'd only ever really seen from a distance were no longer so far away. "Wow, Lulu's never gonna believe this! Even she's never been this close to a mountain before."

Franklin wished he could feel as enthusiastic as Oliver sounded. But he was dizzy and his fur was damp and he wanted nothing more than to be dry and on land again.

At last, the current began to slow. They left the rocky, turbulent ride behind them as the river widened and the waters grew calmer. Franklin sighed with relief and did his best to shake the water from his fur while keeping his balance.

"Look, Franklin!" Oliver said, pointing. "Is that the farmer's market?"

Even before he looked, Franklin knew it wasn't the farmer's market. The smells were completely different here, and the mountains were so close . . . Deep down, Franklin knew that he was farther away from home right now than he had ever been.

But when he saw what Oliver was pointing at, he felt a surge of hope. It was a white boat, long and flat, with two decks and a great big wheel spinning slowly on the back. Franklin knew exactly what it was, because he had seen it before.

"That's a ferryboat!" he exclaimed, tail swishing. "I've been on one before—Lucy and her mom took me!"

"Really?" Oliver perked up. "Do you think they're there now?"

Franklin was getting more excited by the second. "Maybe! There are lots of boats where we live. Sometimes I can even see them from the living room window."

Forget the farmer's market. The ferryboat might actually get Franklin closer to home!

"We need to get on board." Franklin was already sticking a paw in the water and paddling to help the raft along. "It looks like people are getting on it—see them walking up that ramp? But the ferryboat will leave soon!"

Oliver hopped into the water and moved behind it. He grabbed onto the back end with his front paws and kicked his back legs, and soon they were moving at a steady pace toward the ferryboat.

"There's just one thing," Oliver called as he paddled. "Aren't people going to think it's weird when they see an otter and a dog getting on the boat?"

Franklin had already thought of that. "Don't worry," he said, grinning. "I think I have a plan."

13

 **OLIVER**

Oliver pulled the raft to land with only a little bit of reluctance. Franklin hopped off and sprinted for dry sand, tail wagging furiously. He staggered a little bit, and Oliver laughed.

"Are you okay?"

Franklin spun in a circle. "A little dizzy, but I don't care. I'm *so* glad to be on land again!"

Oliver felt slightly bad for taking Franklin on the raft. Not that he'd had any idea it would turn into such a wild ride! Truth be told, Oliver had sort of enjoyed it, even if it was a little bit scary. Maybe he wasn't such a momma otter's boy after all.

Momma. Suddenly, Oliver whirled around and stared at the water.

"It's not black," he said.

"What?" Franklin tilted his head.

"The water isn't black here," Oliver said. "The stream wasn't taking us to the ocean. It was taking us farther away!"

An enormous sadness threatened to engulf Oliver as he sat heavily on the sand.

"I thought Lulu's momma knew everything," he said miserably. "But maybe she didn't."

"What do you mean?" Franklin sat next to him. "She said water is connected to water. She was right—the stream was connected to the river. It *was* connected to another water, just not the water we wanted."

Oliver buried his face in his paws. "This is all my fault! Now I'm farther away from home than ever. And so are you."

"That's why we've gotta get on that ferryboat!" Franklin leaped back to his feet. "Lucy and her mom take boats like that all the time. They might be on that one right now! And even if they're not, that boat might take us to the ocean!"

"I guess so." Oliver glanced at the ferryboat in the distance. Racing through river rapids was one thing. Getting on a boat with people was quite another. "But how am I going to get on without people noticing me?"

"Give me a sec!" Franklin was darting here and there, sniffing frantically. The sand was littered with rocks and damp branches and long leaves that had fallen off the massive trees that lined the beach. Oliver watched as Franklin picked up two particularly muddy leaves between his teeth, then trotted back.

"Here you go!" Franklin said triumphantly after setting the leaves down. "Ears!"

"Ears?" Oliver repeated.

Franklin gave his head an extra-hard shake so that his long ears flopped from side to side. "Dachshund ears! It's a disguise!"

Oliver picked up one of the muddy leaves and

eyed it doubtfully. "I'm not sure this'll make me look like a dachshund," he said.

"It'll work if no one looks too closely," Franklin replied with complete confidence. "I remember being on a boat like this before. Everyone is too busy staring at the water and the mountains to look down at their feet."

"Hmm." Oliver tentatively laid the leaf over the top of his head so that it flopped over on the right. Then he laid the other leaf down so that it flopped over on the left. He pressed down firmly on the leaves, the mud squelching into his scalp, and let go. "They're sticking!"

"Told ya!" Franklin beamed. "You look . . . well, you don't exactly look like a dachshund. But you don't look like an otter, either. Good enough!"

"Good enough." Feeling a little bit better, Oliver followed Franklin down the beach toward the steamship.

"Try not to arch your back so much," Franklin suggested.

Oliver grimaced and attempted to flatten himself so that his back was straight, like Franklin's. He waddled precariously, and his left "ear" flopped over his eyes. "Ack!" he said, brushing it back. "This is kind of hard."

"All you have to do is make it up the ramp," Franklin said. "Then you can hide while I look for Lucy."

"Okay."

They reached the ramp and hung back by the pier, watching as people made their way onto the boat. Oliver was relieved to see that Franklin was right—everyone was chatting and laughing and gazing out at the water. There were even a few dogs! One older man had a big gold-and-black dog with pointy ears wearing some sort of harness, and another woman carried a tiny dog with a very flat face in her arms.

"Here," Franklin said softly, ducking behind a wooden pole. Oliver joined him, crouching low and peering around the pole. Only a few feet away were three pairs of legs, but the people attached to them were leaning against the railing and looking out at the bay.

"Why are we waiting?" Oliver asked anxiously.

"To find some people to walk with," Franklin replied, as if it was the most obvious thing in the world.

"What?"

"We have to look like we're pets," Franklin explained. "We can't just board all by ourselves. We should—"

"Psst!"

Franklin and Oliver glanced up, startled. A dog about Franklin's size was standing right next to their pole! Oliver saw a leash that extended from her collar all the way up to her owner's hand.

"Hi!" Franklin exclaimed, and Oliver fought the urge to hush him. "Are you riding the ferryboat, too?"

"I think so," the dog replied. She had long, fluffy white-and-brown fur and round black eyes. "Did I hear you say you're trying to sneak on?"

"No," Oliver said just as Franklin replied, "Yup!"

The dog narrowed her eyes at Oliver. "You aren't a dog," she said flatly.

Oliver sighed, feeling suddenly ridiculous with his fake muddy ears. "No. I'm an otter. My name's Oliver."

"And I'm Franklin," Franklin added. "I got lost and I think my owner might be on that boat. Can we pretend to be with you and your owners to get on board?"

"Sure," the dog replied with a shrug. "But I don't think anyone's going to believe that otter's a dog."

"Really?" Franklin replied, looking wide-eyed at Oliver. "I think he looks pretty . . . Oh, your right ear is crooked."

Oliver flushed, attempting to straighten his ear.

"Come on, Jordan!" came a voice from above, and Franklin and Oliver ducked down again. The people set off toward the ramp, Jordan trotting alongside. She glanced over her shoulder and mouthed, *Come on! Hurry!*

Here goes nothing, Oliver thought as he and Franklin scurried after them. They kept up behind Jordan and her humans all the way up the ramp. Oliver heard the distant chatter of more people getting louder and louder, and he reminded himself that it would all be okay once they were on the boat. He would just hide and let Franklin search for Lucy . . .

. . . only it quickly became clear that it wasn't going to be that easy.

"There's no place for me to hide!" Oliver said urgently. The deck was a sea of legs and benches. There were no dark corners, no convenient little holes or anything for an otter to squeeze into. The only bright side was that, as Franklin predicted, pretty much everyone stood near the railings and looked out at the view.

"Hmm," Franklin said, although he didn't look nearly as worried as Oliver. "What about over there, by that man?"

Oliver looked over to where a gangly man with a

white beard sat on a stool, holding some sort of box in his hands. As Oliver watched, he pulled the box apart and it stretched. When he squeezed it back together, a sound came out that made Oliver jump.

The people on board seemed delighted with the noise—a few of them even started dancing. The man continued squeezing the box, and Oliver heard a loud *SLAM!* that made him jump again.

"What was that?"

"The ramp," Franklin explained. "The boat's leaving."

Oliver's heart was racing now. He was trapped on this boat wearing a ridiculous dog disguise! He checked to make sure his ear was straight—the right one kept flopping forward—and moved closer to Franklin.

"What should I do?"

"Hide," Franklin said, as if it was obvious. "Behind that thing."

He gestured to the man with the noisy box again, only this time, Oliver noticed the big black box next to his stool. It was tall enough and long enough to hide Oliver if he crouched down and stayed perfectly still.

"Okay," Oliver whispered back. But he didn't move. Because to get to the man, he had to pass by lots and lots of legs. He just knew someone was going to notice him.

"You'd better hurry," Franklin said urgently.

"I can't walk past all these people!" Oliver felt frozen to the floor. "I just can't!"

"What you need is a distraction."

Oliver and Franklin turned to see Jordan standing there, her fluffy tail high in the air. Her owners stood at the railing facing the water.

"Yes! Brilliant!" Franklin said excitedly. "What kind of distraction?"

Jordan tilted her head at him and raised an eyebrow. She didn't respond, but Franklin suddenly went very, very still. Oliver had the sense that they were somehow communicating, even though they weren't talking. He backed away one step, then another.

"ARF-ARF-ARF-ARF-ARF-ARF-ARF!"

Oliver turned and scrambled away as the two dogs began barking at each other simultaneously. He heard Jordan's owner gasp and shout her name, and a few people turned to watch the spectacle. *It's working!* Oliver thought. *No one's looking at me!*

He dove behind the black case and huddled as low as he could, panting. The cacophony had finally subsided, and he heard people laughing. Then someone said, "Who's this little guy's owner, anyway?"

Uh-oh. Was Franklin in trouble?

Throughout all the noise, the man had continued to squeeze the box. He hadn't noticed Oliver yet, and Oliver couldn't bear not knowing what had happened with Franklin. Slowly, he poked his head over the box . . .

. . . and found himself face-to-face with a tiny human.

The little boy had a piece of green paper clenched in his fist. He dropped it into the box Oliver had been hiding behind, and his pink-cheeked face lit up with delight.

"Doggy!"

Oliver flinched as the little boy reached out and gave him a firm pat on the head. His wonky right "ear" slid off and fell into the case, landing right next to the green piece of paper.

The little boy's eyes widened. "Oh no!"

"Hey, what on earth?"

There was a screeching sound as the man with the box shot off his stool. He stopped squeezing the box, and all heads turned in their direction. Oliver stood there, one muddy leaf dangling off the left side of his head.

A woman let out a little shriek and rushed forward, scooping up the little boy. "Timmy, no! That's not a dog! It's . . . What *is* that?"

"It's an otter!" The man with the loud box grinned, shaking his head. "Well, I'll be! There's an otter on this boat!"

Everyone gathered around, and Oliver cowered.

He spotted Franklin making his way through the crowd. The dachshund's eyes were huge, and for once, he seemed at a loss for words.

Oliver could only think of one thing to do. Reaching into his pocket, he pulled out the rocks Franklin had given him.

Then he started to juggle.

LUCY

Lucy trudged into the kitchen and sank down into a chair, dropping her backpack on the floor.

"Let's see, eat first or shower first?" Mom said as she set her keys on the counter. She lifted her arm and pretended to sniff, then wrinkled her nose. "Ew. Probably shower first."

Lucy barely mustered a smile. Once the otter was stable and a few of Mom's coworkers had shown up to help monitor her, they'd headed back to the beach for more cleanup. Lucy thought she could probably shower for an hour and she still wouldn't get the icky smell of oil and sand off her. But she didn't care.

"Oh, hon." Mom sat in the chair opposite her and grabbed her hand. "It's Franklin, isn't it."

"He's been gone for over a day now," Lucy said miserably. She couldn't believe she had to spend a second night without her puppy. "Not a single person has called about the flyers I put out. What if we never find him?"

"We will, sweetie." Mom squeezed her hand. "I'm sorry—I should have helped you look more today."

"No, it's okay," Lucy said. "So many other animals need help right now. And Franklin's missing, but he's not in danger like they are." *I hope,* she added fervently in her head.

"He's going to turn up," Mom said. "I just know it." She got to her feet and started rummaging around the pantry. "How does some mac 'n' cheese sound?"

"Fine."

"Mind if I put the news on?"

"Nah."

Mom slipped her iPad out of its cover and propped it up on the windowsill. The intro music for the local news station filled the kitchen as Mom busied herself boiling water and shredding cheese.

"Cleanup is under way after a minor oil spill in Puget Sound last night. A small tanker began leaking oil around nine thirty p.m. near Bainbridge Island . . ."

Lucy gazed at the images on the iPad, barely listening to the anchors as they reported the spill. After a minute, she pulled out her phone and opened her YouTube app. The first video to pop up in her feed was from ABZ Tours, uploaded only an hour ago.

With a quick glance at Mom, Lucy silenced her phone and watched the video on mute. The first two minutes were drone footage of the spill, and it brought tears to Lucy's eyes. Mom and Ellen had talked about the latest news that afternoon—how the oil spill apparently could have been a lot worse, how only a fraction of the tanker's oil had actually leaked. But still, the sight of the shoreline covered in murky black was devastating.

Lucy was so lost in thought, it was a few seconds before she realized the footage had changed and she was now staring at a familiar furry face.

She sat up, barely managing to stifle a gasp. It was Franklin! For a second, she wondered if Zach had found him—then she realized this was the video she had sent him earlier that day.

True to his word, Zach had included Franklin in the video. Quickly, Lucy scrolled down, then wiggled a little in her chair. The video already had almost a thousand views! Almost a thousand people who now knew what Franklin looked like and where he had been lost.

Maybe there was hope after all!

Lucy continued to scroll down, scanning the comments. They were all about the oil spill, remarks about how upsetting it was, questions about how to help or where to donate. Nothing about Franklin. Sighing, she set her phone down.

"And now, here's Jessica with the lighter side of the news."

A woman with dark red hair and a wide smile appeared on the iPad screen. *"Thanks, Miguel. After a break-in early this morning, the owner of Carl's Clams reviewed the security footage—and got the surprise of his life. Carl, can you tell us what happened?"*

Lucy watched as a smiling older man with a graying beard appeared next to the reporter. *"Sure thing. Well, I got to the shack this morning and found someone had busted the window open with a rock, then ate about half the clams in our fridge. We've got a security camera, but it's aimed at the cash register, and no money was stolen. Still, we watched the footage since you can see a bit of the kitchen in the background and, well . . . the thief turned out to be an otter!"*

Mom looked up from the stove and started to laugh. "Oh no! That's too funny!"

Lucy couldn't help but giggle, too. As Carl continued talking, black-and-white security-camera footage of the shack filled the screen.

"Tricky little bugger used a rock to break the handle off the fridge. There was another critter in there, too. Harder to

see, but honestly it doesn't look like an otter to me. Kinda looks like a dog, don't you think?"

Lucy stopped laughing. She lunged for the iPad, her nose practically touching the screen as the footage replayed. The otter was clear enough, stuffing his face full of clams. But Carl was right—the other creature definitely wasn't an otter. The picture quality was fuzzy, but Lucy couldn't help thinking it looked like a dachshund.

"Mom!" Lucy yelled so loudly, Mom dropped her spatula. "I think that's Franklin!"

"What?" Mom hurried over as the footage rolled for a third time. In the background, Lucy could hear the news anchors laughing. "Look! Doesn't that look like him?"

"I don't know, Lucy . . ." Mom frowned. "It's really hard to see. I guess it *could* be a dog . . ." She glanced at Lucy and straightened up. "How about I call Carl's Clams? Maybe they can tell us more."

"Yes, please!"

Mom headed over to the table while Lucy watched

the rest of the footage. A moment later, Mom cleared her throat.

"So they have a YouTube channel, huh?"

"What?" Lucy whirled around. "Oh! Uh . . ."

Mom smiled, handing her the phone. "Sorry, I wasn't trying to snoop. I thought this was mine . . . Where *is* my phone?"

"Your back pocket." Lucy tried to sound teasing, but it came out nervous and shaky. She knew she didn't have to feel guilty about watching Zach's videos, but she did all the same.

"Ugh, Earth to Sarah . . ." Rolling her eyes, Mom pulled her phone from her pocket and began swiping. A few moments later, she put it on speakerphone and held it out. Lucy heard the dial tone and held her breath.

"Carl's Clams! Is this for pickup or delivery?" came a chipper voice.

"Neither, actually," Mom said smoothly. "I saw the piece on the news about the otter breaking in this morning."

The woman started laughing. "Isn't it the funniest thing? We've all watched the video at least a dozen times today!"

"The thing is, my daughter and I are looking for our lost dachshund puppy," Mom said. "He ran off at the farmer's market not far from you guys. Have you seen any signs of a dog around the shack?"

"Oh, dear." The woman had stopped laughing. "I'm so sorry to hear that. No, hon, I only saw the security footage. I haven't seen any other dogs around here today. Or otters, for that matter."

"Would you mind keeping an eye out?" Sarah asked. "I can give you my number, if you happen to see him?"

"Of course!"

Lucy's shoulders slumped as she headed back to her seat. Was Franklin really running around with an otter? It was too bizarre to contemplate. This was probably just a dead end.

After a quick dinner, Lucy took a long, hot shower. Even though it was barely past eight o'clock, she put her pajamas on. Between all the cleanup work and her anxiety about Franklin, she was exhausted.

She headed to Mom's room to say goodnight. But just as Lucy went to knock, she heard a voice coming from inside and froze with her fist in the air.

It wasn't Mom's voice. It sounded tinny, like someone was on speakerphone again. Had the lady from the clam shack called back? Lucy pressed her ear to the door and listened hard. No, that wasn't a woman's voice. It was definitely a guy. It was . . . wait.

That was Zach's voice!

Lucy pressed her hand to her mouth. Were Mom and Zach talking on the phone? The idea sent Lucy's emotions whirling. On the one hand, she was thrilled that they might be on speaking terms again. On the other hand, why had Zach called? Was something wrong?

Chewing her lip, Lucy tried to decide what to do. Should she knock and interrupt their conversation? What if Zach hung up?

Then she heard another voice. Not Mom's—in

fact, Mom hadn't said a single word. That was Bryson's voice, Lucy realized. Her confusion only lasted a moment.

Mom wasn't on the phone with Zach. She was watching his videos.

A lump rose up in Lucy's throat. After a few seconds, she backed away quietly and headed up to her room.

Mom missed Zach. And Zach missed her, too. Lucy was sure of it.

Why couldn't they just forgive each other and move on?

15

 **FRANKLIN**

A hush had fallen over the ferryboat. The only sound was the wind and the occasional call of a seagull.

Franklin gaped along with everyone else. Oliver was sitting with his legs sticking straight out, rolling the three rocks Franklin had given him over his belly, his neck, and up and down his arms. Only it didn't even really look like Oliver was moving the rocks. It looked like the rocks had come alive and were rolling all over him!

"Wow!" Jordan said in a hushed voice. "How's he doing that?"

"I have no idea," Franklin admitted. "I can't believe I ever thought he could pass for a dachshund. No way could any dachshund do that!"

"No shih tzu could do it, either," Jordan said.

The crowd was starting to laugh now, and a few of them even cheered. Franklin noticed several people pulling out phones and holding them up the same way Lucy did whenever Franklin did anything she found especially adorable.

"Isn't this amazing?" cooed a woman standing next to Jordan's owner. She glanced down at Franklin and Jordan with a big smile. "His little show even got your pups to stop fighting!"

"The dachshund's not mine," Jordan's owner replied. "I already called Animal Services, actually— he doesn't have a collar. I think he might be a stray. They're going to pick him up when we dock."

"Aw." The woman knelt down and gave Franklin a little scratch beneath the chin. "Poor little guy. Hey, you should mention the otter to Animal Services. Not sure if that's their job, but . . ."

She shrugged as she stood up and walked off. Franklin moved closer to Jordan.

"What's Animal Services?"

"Oh, it's no big deal," Jordan said. "Just people who come get you when you're lost."

"Really?" Franklin was suddenly elated. "They can help me get home?"

"Sure!" Jordan paused, glancing at Franklin's neck. "Well . . . actually I'm not sure. You don't have your tags!"

"Oh, right." Franklin's tail flopped to the floor. "So then what will they do?"

"Find you a new home," Jordan said. "That's what happened with Buttercup—she's a Pomeranian who lives next door to me. She ran away from one home and Animal Services took her to a place with lots of crates and she lived there for a while. Then one day her new owner came and took her home."

"What?!" Franklin yelped. "I don't want a new owner or a new home. I have Lucy!"

He turned back to Oliver, who was still juggling. The otter actually looked as if he was enjoying himself now. Almost everyone on deck was crowded around him, and people coming down the stairs from the top deck were gathering, too, craning their necks and standing on tiptoe to see what all the fuss was about.

"No one's looking at you," Jordan pointed out. "They're all too busy watching Oliver. When the ramp goes down, you could just run off without him."

Franklin shook his head. "I can't. I promised I'd help him find his way home, too."

Besides, the idea of leaving Oliver behind made Franklin sad. *Really* sad. It dawned on Franklin for the first time that if he did find Lucy, and Oliver did find his momma, they would have to say goodbye. His tail drooped at the thought.

The man with the squeeze box started playing music again, and Oliver stood on two legs. He rolled the rocks over his shoulders and across his chest and even over his head! The crowd was really getting into it now, and pretty much no one was looking out at the mountains as they drew closer and closer.

The mountains. Franklin did a double take, staring up at what he could see over the railing. Those were the mountains he'd seen on the other side of the water from the farmer's market. Only now, they were right there.

The ferryboat wasn't taking him home at all. Now he was farther away than ever!

The deep blare of a horn sounded, and Jordan gave Franklin a nervous look. "That means the boat's gonna dock soon."

"I know." Franklin's stomach flipped. He had to get Oliver off this boat, and fast.

He sat next to Jordan, every muscle in his body tensing as the ferryboat slowed its speed. There was a mild bump as it docked, and Franklin knew it was now or never.

"Thanks for all your help!" he whispered to Jordan.

Her fluffy tail swished back and forth. "No problem!"

Franklin hurried over to the gate blocking the entrance to the ramp. He stared at Oliver, willing the otter to see him, but Oliver was too caught up in his juggling routine now. He wasn't paying any attention at all.

Franklin sighed. There was only one thing to do.

"Arf! Arf! ARF-ARF-ARF!"

The moment he started barking, several things happened all at once.

Oliver dropped his rocks in surprise and swiveled around to stare at Franklin.

The man with the squeeze box stopped squeezing.

The people holding out their phones turned to point them at Franklin instead.

And there was a loud *BANG!* as the metal ramp hit the dock and the gate opened.

"Oliver, run! *Now!*" Franklin scurried off down the ramp as fast as his little legs could go. He heard shouts and cries as Oliver scampered after him. A few dockworkers leaped back in shock when a dog and an otter raced off the boat and took off down the beach.

They flew across the pebbly shore, leaping over driftwood and rocks, not daring to look back. Franklin's ears streamed behind him as he ran faster than he'd ever run, even faster than the one time Lucy had taken him to an off-leash park and thrown a Frisbee for him to catch.

Finally, he slowed down and tried to catch his breath.

"Why'd we have to run like that?" Oliver asked between gulps of air.

"Because people were going to take me to Animal Services," Franklin said, sitting on his haunches with his legs sticking out. "That's where lost dogs go to get a new home."

Oliver's eyes went wide. "Oh."

"Going on the boat was a bad idea," Franklin said, hanging his head. "I'm sorry, Oliver. I think we're even farther away from the farmer's market now. I . . . I don't know how to get home."

"It's okay," Oliver said kindly. "We'll come up with a new plan tomorrow."

"Tomorrow?" Franklin looked up and blinked. He'd been so focused on escaping, he hadn't even noticed how low the sun was in the sky. It would be night soon.

Another night without Lucy.

Franklin started to tremble uncontrollably. This had only happened a few times before, when Lucy's mom had been cooking and the fire alarm started blasting its shrill *BEEP BEEP BEEP*. Even after it would stop, Franklin would shake and shake.

There was no fire alarm now, but Franklin was trembling anyway. During the day, there were so many exciting things to distract him from missing Lucy. But he really, *really* didn't want to spend another night outside. And what if he couldn't find Lucy tomorrow, and had to spend *another* night outside? How many nights would it be before Franklin made his way home?

What if he *never* made his way home? That thought was even scarier than the fire alarm.

"I know what'll cheer you up!" Oliver hopped up brightly. "I'll go collect some clams for dinner!"

Franklin tried to smile. "Okay. Thanks."

He had to admit, he was hungry. But he didn't feel cheery as he watched the otter scurry out to the water. He couldn't stop thinking about how careless he'd been, slipping out of his collar and running after that squirrel.

Franklin, you really, really *need to learn how to stay!*

Franklin curled up into a ball and tried really hard to stop trembling. But it was no use.

Lucy was always so worried about him. Now he knew she had a good reason.

"ARF? ARF? ARF? ARF? ARF?"

Franklin bolted upright and promptly bumped his head on the ceiling. Utterly disoriented, he tried to turn around and bumped right into a wall. Where was he? And who was *barking*?

"What is that?" Oliver yelped, his back arched.

Franklin felt all his fur standing on end. The two

of them had fallen asleep inside a giant, hollowed-out driftwood log. And there had been no one, animal or human, on the beach last night.

But now . . .

"ARF? ARF? ARF? ARF? ARF?"

Franklin could feel his instincts taking over. He'd heard all sorts of different dog barks, but he had never *ever* heard anything like this. It sounded like a whole pack of dogs, and their barks were hoarse and sharp and so, so *loud*.

Paws scrabbling against the smooth wood, Franklin raced out of one end of the log and spun around on the sand, looking for the source of the sound.

"ARF? ARF? ARF? ARF? ARF?"

There! Right next to an old, crumbling pier—several of the biggest dogs Franklin had ever seen, lying in the shallow water and barking at top volume.

A low rumble sounded in Franklin's chest. He couldn't help it. Oliver joined him and gasped when he saw the giant dogs.

"Franklin, those are— Wait, stop!"

But it was too late. Franklin raced toward the pack, barking at the top of his lungs.

"Arf-arf-arf-arf-arf-arf-arf-arf-arf-arf!"

For a brief moment, the pack of dogs fell silent. They all turned to face Franklin, wet black noses with long whiskers twitching. Then—

"*ARF? ARF? ARF? ARF? ARF?*"

"*Arf-arf-arf-arf-arf-arf-arf-arf-arf-arf!*"

"*ARF? ARF? ARF? ARF? ARF?*"

"*ARF-ARF-ARF-ARF-ARF-ARF!*"

"Stop! Franklin!" Oliver was next to him, hands clasped over his ears, shaking his head back and forth. But Franklin couldn't stop barking. His tail wagged frantically as the giant dogs started to walk out of the water.

Only they weren't walking.

"*ARF-ARF . . .*" Franklin fell silent mid-bark. The dogs weren't walking. They were flopping from side to side and kind of wiggling their way onto the sand. And they didn't have legs. They had flippers.

Their barking ceased, too, and Oliver lowered his paws with a sigh of relief.

"Those aren't dogs," Franklin said unnecessarily.

Oliver let out a nervous laugh. "Nope. They're sea lions."

Franklin cowered back, tail tucked between his legs, as the sea lions flip-flopped closer and closer. They were even bigger than he'd realized when they were in the water. Way, *way* bigger than any dog. Even bigger than Juno the Great Dane!

The sea lions came to a stop a few feet away, eyeing the otter and the dog suspiciously.

"Good morning," Oliver squeaked. "Um . . . sorry about the noise."

The biggest sea lion peered at him, then at Franklin, who cowered back even more. "No need to apologize," he replied. "That was some impressive barking for such a small . . . land lion?"

Franklin lifted his head slightly. "I'm a dachshund."

The sea lion eyed him appreciatively. "I see. You're quite loud, little one."

"Thank you," Franklin said, pleased.

"What's a sea otter doing with a dachshund?" another sea lion asked curiously. "For that matter, why are you here in the bay at all? I've never seen a sea otter this far from the sea."

"The black water," a third sea lion piped up. "That must be it. Did you get lost, little otter?"

Oliver nodded. "Yes! I ended up on land, and I've been trying to find my—my momma, because I was with her when the water turned black, but . . ."

He trailed off, and Franklin felt a wave of sympathy. The sea lions all lowered their heads.

"I'm so sorry," the largest sea lion said. "Many animals were caught in the black water. We barely managed to make it to the bay ourselves."

"Can you tell us how to get back to the ocean?" Oliver asked desperately. "I need to get home. I need to see if Momma made it back."

The sea lions looked at one another. "The quickest way is the strait, of course," the largest sea lion said slowly. "But that route is contaminated with the black water."

Franklin saw the disappointment all over Oliver's face. But there was something else—that look the sea lions had exchanged. "Is there another way?" Franklin asked.

Those large black eyes all fixed on him.

"There is," the largest sea lion said at last. "Not one that sea lions could ever take, but for you . . ." He turned back to Oliver. "You might be able to do it."

"What is it?" Oliver asked eagerly.

"There is a river that leads out to the sea."

Franklin suppressed a groan, remembering the wild ride on the rapids. But Oliver perked up instantly, looking up and down the beach.

"Is it close by?"

The largest sea lion gestured with his flipper. "Behind you. Somewhere in there."

Oliver and Franklin turned around. Where the beach ended, a forest began, thick and dark and menacing looking, even in the daytime. The forest rose up, and up, and up, the land slowly sloping higher and higher, and in the not-so-far distance, Franklin could see snowy peaks above the tree line.

He turned to Oliver, who didn't look nearly as eager anymore.

"We have to go into the mountains."

16

 OLIVER

Oliver was less than thrilled about being back in the woods.

These woods weren't like the ones he and Franklin had wandered through yesterday. That forest had been bright and sunny, with the trees spread far enough apart so that it still felt spacious.

The trees in this forest were much bigger, much taller, and much, *much* closer together. Even though it was daytime, it almost felt like night inside. And it didn't help that the sky was especially overcast today. The sea lion's words rang over and over again in Oliver's mind, adding to his doom-and-gloom mood.

Many animals were caught in the black water. We barely managed to make it to the bay ourselves.

Oliver almost didn't want to find his way home. Because what if he made it there, and Momma was nowhere to be found? He couldn't bear the thought.

"Ooh, there's a good stick!" Franklin trotted up ahead a few steps and picked up a sturdy-looking stick, tail high in the air.

"What do you need that for?" Oliver asked curiously.

Franklin blinked. "Just to carry."

"Oh."

They continued up the steep path they'd been climbing. Oliver already felt tired and, well, dry. He'd been so eager to find the river that he'd headed straight into the forest after thanking the sea lions. Now, he wished he'd taken a nice bath before leaving the bay behind.

Suddenly, Franklin spat the stick out. "Ooh, look!" he exclaimed, darting beneath a bush. He emerged a moment later with a smooth, flat rock. "Is this like your first rock?"

Oliver took the rock and examined it. "A little, although mine was pointier on one end. But this is really nice!" he added quickly, tucking the rock into his pocket.

In their haste to leave the ferryboat, Oliver had left all of the rocks Franklin had given him behind. Not that it mattered. None of them had been quite right. Neither was this one, but Oliver didn't want to hurt Franklin's feelings. And having a rock tucked into his pocket again was a nice comfort.

A few minutes later, Franklin stopped walking, his ears perking up.

Oliver stopped, too. "What is it? Do you hear the river?" he asked hopefully.

"No . . ." Franklin's eyes darted this way and that. "I thought I heard something, but maybe I imagined it."

They continued walking, but stopped less than a

minute later. He lifted his nose in the air and took a deep sniff.

"Do you smell the river?" Oliver asked, although he was starting to get a bad feeling in the pit of his belly.

"No . . ." Franklin turned in a slow circle. "But I do smell . . . something. An animal."

Please, please don't be a squirrel, Oliver thought desperately. The idea of Franklin running off, of being alone in this dark, scary forest, was more than he could handle.

"What should we do?" he asked after a moment.

Franklin turned around once more. "Keep walking. Only . . . let's go this way."

Oliver dutifully followed Franklin off the bumpy, rocky path they'd been climbing and into the thick cluster of trees. His heart was pounding hard now. What had Franklin smelled? What kinds of animals lived in the woods? Oliver searched his mind for stories from Lulu's momma. She knew something about the forests—she'd visited a waterfall before where some distant cousins lived. Oliver and Lulu had loved those stories.

Oliver tried to focus on the amazing stories he'd have to tell when he got home. Only now, even he could smell what Franklin smelled. The scent of something big and furry.

There was a rustling behind them, and Oliver began to move faster. Franklin kept up at a brisk trot. The two glanced at each other but said nothing.

They climbed over a thick, gnarled root and then squeezed between two moss-covered rocks. The rustling had stopped. The trees were suddenly very, very still.

Oliver wriggled under a bush and stood up—and froze.

Franklin popped up next to him. "What are you . . . *Oh.*"

Only a few feet away stood what Oliver first thought was the largest dog in the whole world. It had brown fur, like Franklin, but its ears were short and round. It had a black nose and black eyes and extremely sharp claws.

It locked eyes with Oliver. Then, slowly, it stood up on hind legs.

Suddenly, Oliver heard Lulu's hushed voice in his mind: *My momma says that our cousins who live by the waterfall all know not to go too deep into the woods, because they might meet a* bear.

A bear? little Oliver had replied in awe. *What's a bear?*

It's a giant animal with teeth like a shark! Lulu informed, and Oliver had gasped. *My cousin Mirabelle saw one once and thought it was going to* eat *her. But she didn't run away, because she knew the bear would catch her. So she just stayed real, real still, and the bear left her alone.*

"That's the biggest dog I've ever seen," Franklin said wonderingly. "Let's ask him to help us! I bet he can sniff out *anything*!"

"No!" Oliver grabbed Franklin by the scruff before he could run up to the bear, who was still standing there, eyeing them. "It's too dangerous!"

"Dangerous?" Franklin sounded skeptical. "Why? Just because he's big?"

"Because he's a *bear.*"

"Are bears dangerous?"

"Yes!"

"How do you know?" Franklin asked. "Have you met one before?"

"Well, no, but . . ." Oliver stopped when the bear dropped back to all fours with a great *thud* that seemed to shake the forest. He continued staring at Oliver and Franklin. He didn't look angry, but he didn't exactly look friendly, either.

"I think we should ask the bear for help," Franklin said stubbornly. "You don't know he's dangerous."

"You don't know he's not!" Oliver hissed, frustration bubbling up in his chest. "Don't do it, Franklin!"

Franklin looked frustrated, too. "You can't tell me what to do."

Then he faced the bear and began to bark.

"Arf-arf! Arf-arf!"

"Noooo," Oliver pleaded, but it was too late.

The bear took a slow, almost lazy step forward. It took every ounce of willpower Oliver had not to run away as fast as he could when the bear took another step forward, then a third. Two more steps, and now it towered over them.

Franklin didn't look scared, but he stopped barking. And to Oliver's surprise, he stayed silent.

Even when the bear leaned down.

Even when the bear's nose appeared right in front of their faces.

Even when the bear took a great, long *sniiiiiiiiff!* that caused their whiskers to tremble.

Oliver didn't breathe. He didn't move a muscle.

Slowly, the bear backed up. Then, with a disinterested grunt, it lumbered off into the trees.

Neither Oliver nor Franklin moved until the *boom-boom-boom* of the bear's steps had faded away. Then Oliver sat down hard.

"Why did you do that?" he cried shakily. "That bear could've— It might have—"

"It didn't do anything!" Franklin sounded cross. "I told you so."

"Look, if we're going to stay together, you have to

promise not to go talking to every animal we see," Oliver said sternly. "You have to trust me. I know what's best for you, and—"

You have to trust me, sweetie. I know what's best for you.

Oliver stood there, mouth slightly open as he remembered Olympia chiding him yesterday.

Franklin's ears flattened. "You do not know what's best for me," he said, and Oliver could tell he'd hurt the puppy's feelings. "So maybe we'd better not stay together at all."

"Wait, Franklin!" Oliver cried, but his friend was already racing deeper into the forest.

17

 **LUCY**

Lucy found Mom in the kitchen the next morning, pouring her coffee into a thermos.

"Morning, sweetie," Mom said. She sounded distracted as she added a splash of half-and-half to the thermos. "I've got to get to the lab—will you be okay on your own for breakfast?"

"Um. Actually." Lucy clutched her phone, struggling to sound normal. "I didn't want to sit around here all day—I mean, I want to look for Franklin around the clam shack, and help with the beach cleanup, so I . . . um, I texted—"

A knock at the door cut her off. Lucy met Mom's

gaze and saw her expression go from confused to more of a *what-have-you-done-now* kind of look.

"I texted Zach," Lucy finished, her voice squeaking slightly on her brother's name.

Mom's face went blank. "Ah."

She busied herself with her coffee again, and Lucy hurried into the living room. She tried not to think of how ridiculous it was that her brother was knocking on the door. Like a visitor, not a member of the family who'd lived here his whole life. Sighing, Lucy opened the front door.

"Hey, Luce." Zach smiled tightly at her, but he made no move to step inside. "Ready?"

Lucy swallowed hard. "No, I need to get the flyers. Um . . ."

She stepped back, holding the door open. Surely he wasn't going to just stand there on the front porch and wait?

Zach exhaled loudly and stuffed his hands in his pockets. "Yeah, no problem," he said, stepping inside.

Lucy's stomach flip-flopped as she crossed the

living room again. Just as she passed the kitchen door, Mom stepped out, cradling her thermos in her hands.

Suddenly, Lucy regretted inviting her brother inside. The last time the three of them had all been in this house together had been the final fight. The big one that had ended with Zach throwing all his stuff in a bag and leaving the house for good.

"Hi," Mom said. Her expression was unreadable now.

Zach shifted from foot to foot, his eyes darting all over the living room. "Hey."

Lucy hated the way her pulse was racing so fast. She hated how all her muscles were tense, waiting for the shouting to start again. That had been her reality all last spring, and it was exhausting. She hurried down the hallway. *Just get Zach out of here before they can start arguing.*

In her bedroom, Lucy threw her water bottle and the few flyers she had left into her backpack. When she stepped back into the hall, she heard voices.

Not shouting voices. Talking voices.

Feeling tentatively hopeful, Lucy returned to the living room just as Mom said:

"I watched a few of your videos last night. That was really smart, using your tour boat as a skimmer. And your coverage of the oil spill was really good."

Zach looked as surprised as Lucy felt. "Really? I mean, thanks!" he said, sounding uncertain. "Bryson's the videographer, though. I run the tours."

"And how's that going?" Mom asked.

Lucy held her breath as Zach responded.

"Good. Really good. Things got off to a slow start in June, but by August we were booking about ten excursions a week. September's looking even better . . ." Zach paused, wrinkling his nose. "Well, it was until this oil spill. Lots of cancellations."

Mom sighed and shook her head. "That's too bad. But that kind of thing happens when you try and run a business."

"What's that supposed to mean?" Zach's face had gone slightly pink.

Oh no, Lucy thought.

"It means running a business isn't all sunshine and roses," Mom said with a shrug. "I mean, you just said you're not making any money next month—"

"I didn't say that!"

"You said there were lots of cancellations."

"Yeah, but we still have sponsorship money."

"And how long do you think that will last?" Mom sighed again. "See, this is exactly what I kept trying to explain to you, but you thought you knew better. Something can happen—something like an oil spill—and your business is gone, and you've got nothing to fall back on."

"Right." Zach's cheeks were tomato red now. "I'd be much better off sitting in some classroom right now racking up student loans instead of actually—"

"*Stop!*"

Zach and Mom turned to stare at Lucy. It was as if they had forgotten her presence—which was exactly what always happened when they argued.

Lucy took a deep breath. Her eyes felt hot, but she managed to hold back her tears.

"You guys keep having the same fight over and over again," she said in a loud, clear voice. "If you don't want to be a family anymore, I can't do anything about that. But please stop yelling at each other when I'm around."

Mom looked stunned. "Lucy, I—"

"I have to go look for Franklin," Lucy said, marching across the living room. "Bye, Mom."

"Lucy—"

But Lucy was already out the front door.

Carl's Clams didn't open till noon, but Lucy had been prepared for that. The moment her brother parked, she hopped out of his car and went straight to the walk-up counter. The gate was pulled down and locked, but there was still room on the counter for her flyers.

She set them in a neat stack, then placed the letter she'd written that morning on top. Then she pulled out a roll of tape and secured the corners to the counter.

"What's that?" Zach said, coming up next to her and peering at the letter. It was the first he'd spoken since they'd left the house.

"I wanted to explain that these flyers are about the dachshund in their security footage, and to ask them to hang them up and ask their customers if they've seen him," Lucy explained.

"Smart," Zach chuckled. "I'd love to see that footage. An otter breaking into a clam shack is pretty hilarious."

Lucy tried to smile. But between the tension of that morning and her anxiety over Franklin, it was hard to fake amusement. Over the last two days, Lucy had felt like a rubber band being pulled tighter and tighter. And this morning, she had snapped.

She couldn't believe she'd said all that to Mom and Zach. They'd both looked so shocked. And why wouldn't they be? In all the months of arguments before Zach left, Lucy had never once yelled like that. She'd tried to stay out of sight, to keep the peace.

It had been easier then, because she had Franklin to listen to her and comfort her. But now . . .

Sighing, Lucy left the flyers taped to the counter and turned to look at the beach. Her heart lurched at the sight of the rocks all slick and black with oil. She thought about the otter recovering at her mother's lab . . . and then she thought about the otter that smashed the window of the clam shack. That poor otter had probably washed up on this very beach!

"Hey, Luce? Come look at this!"

Turning, Lucy followed the sound of Zach's voice and hurried around the north side of the shack. He was standing beneath a pipe shower, which made Lucy smile for real.

"Did you forget to shower this morning?"

Zach rolled his eyes. "Very funny. Look at the concrete!"

Lucy stepped forward and looked at the circular slab of concrete. In the center was a drain. And surrounding the drain were oily paw prints.

Her pulse quickened. "Those don't look like dog prints," she said, although her heart had lifted at the sight of them.

"Nope." Zach pointed to the handle at the base of the pipe. "But those do."

Lucy gasped when she saw the black paw prints. "You're right! Those could be Franklin's paw prints! And these . . ." Lucy stared down at the odd prints again. "Do you think . . ."

"They belong to an otter?" Zach grinned and shook his head. "That'd be wild. Did the shack worker mention oily prints in the kitchen?"

"No." Lucy paused. "But if he rinsed off before he broke in . . ."

She trailed off, meeting her brother's gaze. Then they both started to laugh.

"So Franklin helped an otter take a shower then break into a restaurant and pig out on clams. Is that what we're thinking?"

Lucy could hardly breathe, she was laughing so hard. "No!" she managed to say. It was ridiculous and she knew it.

"Hey, listen," Zach said, and something about his frown made Lucy stop laughing. "About this morning . . . with Mom. I'm sorry about that."

Lucy gazed at him. "For what, exactly?"

"For, you know . . ." Zach shrugged helplessly. "Arguing. Stressing you out."

Now it was Lucy's turn to roll her eyes. "You think that's why I'm upset?"

"Well . . . yeah."

"Mom misses you," Lucy told him. "Why else do you think she stayed up watching your videos? She misses you. It hurt her feelings when you left. And . . . and mine, too."

Lucy pressed her lips together. She hadn't meant to say that. She hadn't even really been thinking it. But once the words were out, she realized they were true.

Zach's mouth opened and closed a few times. "I wasn't leaving *you*, Luce," he said finally. "You know that, right?"

"Except that's exactly what you did." Lucy looked down at her shoes. "You left home. And I know we text all the time, but that's not the same. I miss you."

"I miss you, too," Zach said quietly, and Lucy glanced up. "And . . . and maybe I do miss Mom. But she's just so judgmental! She thinks she knows best about everything, especially college."

"She was just worried about you," Lucy mumbled.

"I know that," Zach said. "Seriously, Luce. But the thing is, I listened to her. I really thought a lot about this decision. I did my own research and I decided college wasn't for me. But every time I tried to explain that to her, she'd just start going on and on about how I was being immature, making rash decisions." He sighed heavily. "Everyone makes mistakes, right? Maybe this *was* a mistake. But if it was, well, at least I tried. At least I followed my heart. Does that make any sense at all?"

Lucy nodded. "Yeah. It really does. And for what it's worth, I think ABZ Tours is awesome."

"Thanks, Luce." Zach's phone buzzed, and his eyes widened when he looked at the screen. "Oh, hang on . . . it's a message from Bryson: 'Is this Franklin?'"

Lucy's heart leaped into her throat. "He found him?" she cried, hurrying over to see the screen. Bryson's message was accompanied by a link to a

YouTube video, and she watched Zach open it. The title was "Best Busker in Seattle?"

"Is this on your channel?" Lucy asked breathlessly as they waited for the video to begin.

Zach shook his head. "Nope. Wow, look—uploaded last night and it's already got over twenty thousand views!"

He fell silent as the video began. It was a shaky phone recording of an accordionist. The person holding the phone was trying to make his way to the front of a crowd of people, and Lucy caught glimpses of benches, sky, and water—a ferry, or some sort of boat, she thought.

When the person reached the front of the crowd, he zoomed in not on the accordionist, but on the animal at his feet.

"Is that . . ." Zach trailed off, but Lucy finished the sentence.

"An otter!"

Lucy had seen otters at the zoo juggle rocks before. But she'd never seen one put on this kind of performance. This otter was rolling rocks over his shoulders, up and down his legs, lying on his back and sending one from the top of his head to the tip of his paws then back again.

"He's amazing!" Lucy said. "But why did Bryson think—"

She stopped short when shouts came from the crowd on the video. It happened very quickly: The person holding the phone swiveled away from the otter and ran toward the ramp. A moment later, another creature flew down the ramp in a blur of brown fur. But this was no otter.

"That's Franklin!" Lucy cried, clapping her hand to her mouth.

She and Zach stared as the otter sped down the ramp after Franklin. The person holding the phone kept the camera on them as they sped off down the beach and vanished from sight.

Zach lowered his phone, and he and Lucy stared at each other in amazement. "I can't believe it," Lucy said slowly. Then she groaned, closing her eyes.

"Franklin was right there around all those people. If only he had his collar on! Someone probably would have called us. Now we still have no idea where he is."

"Not true." Zach scrolled down to the description of the video and read aloud, "'This otter's got a future in show business! Took the Dabob Bay ferryboat today and caught this amazing performance. A few people called Animal Services, but as you can see, the otter took off like a true rock star who doesn't want to stick around and chat with his adoring fans. To make it even weirder, there was a stray dog on the ship and the two ran off together!'"

Lucy still couldn't believe Franklin was running around with an otter. But that wasn't the part she was focused on now. "Dabob Bay? Where's that?"

Zach was already opening his maps app. "It's . . . No, that can't be right. I must be mixing it up with . . ." He typed the words into the search box, and Lucy leaned forward as the map zoomed in on a strip of blue water labeled Dabob Bay.

"Zoom out!" she said eagerly, and Zach did. But

Lucy didn't recognize any of the surrounding towns or bays. He zoomed out again, and again, revealing more canals and bays and peninsulas and then finally, Whidbey Island.

Lucy stared from the island where she lived, to Puget Sound, to the peninsula with the Kingston farmer's market, to Dabob Bay. The marina was on the west side of the bay, and behind it, the enormous mass of green land covered in mountains. Lucy knew exactly where it was before she read the label.

"Olympic National Park," Zach said, sounding stunned. "How in the world did Franklin get all the way over there?"

Lucy closed her eyes, but all she could see was hundreds of acres of mountainous rain forests. If Franklin really was in Olympic National Park, there was no way she'd ever find him.

FRANKLIN

Franklin raced through the woods as fast as he could. Distantly, he heard Oliver calling out behind him, but now that he'd started running, he couldn't stop.

"Franklin! *Franklin!*"

This is what got you into this situation in the first place, said a voice in Franklin's head. *Do you want to lose Oliver the way you lost Lucy?*

Franklin gritted his teeth and forced himself to slow down. He was frustrated with Oliver, but maybe he was also frustrated with himself a little bit. After all, Oliver could have been right. The bear *could* have been dangerous.

For a moment, all Franklin could hear was the sound of his own panting.

Then, another sound. A wonderfully familiar sound.

Water.

Franklin spun around, ears alert, trying to figure out the direction it was coming from. It was close, *very* close, yet all he could see were trees.

"Oliver!" he called. "Oliver, over here!"

A few seconds later, there was a rustling sound. Then the otter squirmed out from under a bush. When he spotted Franklin, his shoulders slumped with relief.

"There you are! I was—"

"Listen!"

Oliver fell silent, and a moment later, his face lit up. "That sounds like a river!"

"But why can't we see it?" Slowly, Franklin continued in the direction he'd been running. He could smell it now, that fresh, slightly fishy river scent, and the sound was growing louder—water rushing over rocks, splashing and slapping against a shore.

But Franklin was moving uphill, and he saw nothing except for trees! Confused, he picked up speed, hurrying around a fallen trunk and scrambling over a root and then—

"Look out!"

One moment, Franklin's front paws were on solid ground. The next moment, the ground was gone! Franklin flailed helplessly, trying to back up, but he felt himself tip forward and start to fall.

Oliver grabbed Franklin's tail in the nick of time. He pulled Franklin back, and they both stared at the sight below them.

They were standing on the edge of a gorge, a sheer, rocky drop that made Franklin dizzy. At the bottom was a river, and the waters were so clear that Franklin could see lots of large, silvery fish swimming upstream. The river itself was surprisingly calm, and Franklin saw the source of the rushing, splashing, slapping sounds at once.

Directly across the gorge was a waterfall!

"Wow," Franklin said, watching the foamy white spray as the water hit the rocks.

"I'll say." Oliver looked at Franklin with wide eyes. "If you hadn't stopped running, you would've run right off the edge and fallen into the river!"

Franklin blinked. He hadn't even considered that. But he really wasn't in the mood for another lecture from Oliver.

"Well, the good news is that the sea lions said this river leads to the ocean!" Franklin said, deciding to change the subject. "But how will we get down there?"

"Good question."

They looked left and right, but Franklin couldn't see any possible way they could climb down. And even if they could, there was no shore on this side of the river, just slippery-looking rocks.

"Look!" Oliver said, hurrying over to a tree on the other side of Franklin. The tree was so close to the edge of the gorge, some of its roots stuck out of the ground and dangled over the edge. The tree itself tilted over the gorge, thick branches stretching down like a hand reaching for the river.

"What are you doing?" Franklin asked uncertainly as Oliver climbed the trunk.

"This branch hangs really low," Oliver said, carefully navigating his way onto a sturdy, thick branch. "If we can climb to the bottom, it won't be a far drop into the river. Then we can swim to the other . . . Oh." He paused, looking back at Franklin. "I forgot you can't swim."

Franklin wrinkled his nose. "I *can* swim. I just don't *like* to swim."

"Well . . ." Oliver glanced down at the river. "It would only be a few seconds! The river's not very wide. Then we'll be on the other side and we can follow it out to the ocean!"

Franklin wanted to say no, but Oliver was right—this was the only way to get to the river.

"Okay," he said at last, tentatively stepping onto the slanted trunk.

Oliver was much better at climbing than Franklin, and as their combined weight caused the branch to sag, Franklin stumbled. Oliver grabbed his tail again and held it tight.

"You lead, I'll follow," Oliver said. "I'll hang on to your tail, okay?"

Franklin couldn't speak. The branch had felt so sturdy a second ago, but now, with the gorge and the river below him, Franklin felt like he was standing on a twig.

He inched forward step by step, Oliver right behind him. The branch sagged heavily, and Franklin let out a whimper as they tilted forward until they were facing straight down. He was grateful for the tight grip Oliver had on his tail.

"Keep going!" Oliver said. "As far down the branch as we can, then we'll jump."

Franklin obeyed, trying to focus on the branch and not the water below him. The branch grew thinner with every step, shaking precariously under the weight of the two animals—and then, a second before it happened, Franklin could tell the branch couldn't hold them any longer.

"Look out!" was all he managed to cry before the end of the branch snapped and he and Oliver plummeted into the river.

It was only a few feet, but Franklin hit the water with a mighty splash. He paddled his legs as hard as he could, but he kept sinking. The river looked fairly calm on top, but underneath it was moving *fast*. Franklin tumbled tail over snout until he had no idea which way the surface was—and then, a furry, whiskery face appeared in front of him.

An otter . . . but it wasn't Oliver.

The otter's paws latched on to Franklin's fur and pulled. They broke the surface, and Franklin gasped for breath as the otter pulled him to shore.

He collapsed on the pebbles, panting and looking around in confusion. The waterfall was in the distance—the river had carried him farther than he'd realized! Franklin stood up and gave himself a good shake. Then he realized he was surrounded by otters.

Franklin turned in a slow circle, hackles rising slightly. These otters were all smaller than Oliver, and their fur was a little bit darker. Not far away was a pile of those big silvery fish, and Franklin realized they must have been catching their lunch when they found him.

"Franklin? Franklin!"

Franklin and the otters all turned in unison to the river. Oliver's head poked up out of the water, and his face lit up when he saw Franklin.

Then he saw the otters, and his jaw dropped.

Franklin felt a wave of relief as Oliver swam to shore and joined them. The otters seemed to relax, too.

"Hello!" Oliver said. "Thanks for rescuing my friend."

"Of course," said the otter who had pulled Franklin from the river. Her whiskers twitched slightly as she turned to Franklin. "You're a dog, right?"

"I'm a dachshund," Franklin said proudly. "My name is Franklin."

"I'm Mirabelle," the otter replied. "No offense, but you're a terrible swimmer!"

She said it kindly, and Franklin laughed. He was about to explain what he and Oliver had been doing, when Oliver suddenly cried out:

"You're Mirabelle?"

Mirabelle turned to him in surprise. "Yes. Why?"

"I'm Oliver," Oliver said eagerly. "Your cousin Lulu is my best friend!"

"Oh, wow!" Mirabelle beamed at him. "I haven't seen Lulu in a long time. Goodness, what are you doing so far from the ocean?"

Oliver and Franklin exchanged a look.

"It's a long story," Oliver said.

"A very long story," Franklin added. He was about to say more when his stomach rumbled.

Mirabelle giggled. "How about we have some lunch and you tell us all about it?"

"That would be great!" Oliver said. He hesitated a moment, then added: "Is it true this river leads to the ocean?"

"It sure does!" Mirabelle replied immediately. "That's the route I take to visit Lulu."

Oliver cheered, and Franklin let out a happy bark. They'd done it! They really were going to find their way to the ocean.

But as Franklin followed the otters to the fish pile, he couldn't help but wonder what would happen after that. Because Oliver would be home, but Franklin would be farther away from home—and from Lucy— than ever.

19

 OLIVER

Oliver couldn't believe it. He was having lunch with river otters! Wait until he told Lulu he'd gone far enough inland to meet her cousins. Even Lulu had never gone on an adventure this epic before.

The fresh salmon was delicious, and Oliver couldn't eat enough. Franklin seemed to be enjoying his meal, too, although Oliver noticed the dachshund was being unusually quiet. Maybe he just felt out of place among all the otters.

More likely, Oliver thought sadly, he was thinking about Lucy.

This whole time, their plan had been to find Lucy

and her mom in the hopes that they would bring Oliver home. Instead, now Oliver was going to go home . . . but where would that leave Franklin? Oliver thought about what Franklin had said about something called Animal Services and finding a new home. His heart broke when he thought about the cheerful, hyper dachshund getting sent off to live with strangers.

When they finished eating, the otters bustled around tidying up the fish bones. Oliver got up and went to sit next to Franklin.

"I'm sorry about what I said earlier," Oliver told him. "About the bear. You were right—he wasn't dangerous."

Franklin's tail thumped once against the pebbles. "He might've been, though."

"I guess." Oliver took a deep breath. "But I shouldn't have ordered you around like that. I shouldn't have said I know what's best. That's . . . that's what my mom says to me all the time. Actually . . ." His eyes felt hot, and he looked down at his paws. "It's what she said right before I tried swimming to Puget Sound and got lost. I really should've listened to her."

Franklin tilted his head. "Why didn't you?"

"Same reason you didn't listen to me," Oliver said with a shrug. "I was annoyed. I thought she was just trying to stop me from having fun. I . . . I was tired of her treating me like a baby."

"Lucy does that, too, sometimes," Franklin said.

"Did it annoy you?"

Franklin looked surprised by the question. "No!"

"Really?" Oliver stared at the dachshund. His brown eyes were wide and solemn.

"Really. I know Lucy only says that stuff because she doesn't want me to get in trouble." Franklin sighed heavily. "I wish I'd listened to her, too."

Oliver felt a pang in his chest as he pictured Olympia's round face filled with worry. "Yeah."

"But you know what?" Franklin said, his ears perking up. "If I hadn't run after the squirrel and you hadn't tried to swim to Puget Sound, we never would've met!"

Oliver grinned, his spirits lifting slightly. "That's true."

"Ready to build a raft?" Mirabelle called from the water's edge.

Oliver stood, brushing a few pebbles from his fur. "Actually, we were going to walk."

"Really? Why?" Mirabelle asked. "It'll take so much longer that way! If you take a raft, you'll be at the ocean before the sun goes down."

Oliver's heart sped up at the thought. Home! *Today!*

"We made a raft yesterday, but, well . . ." Oliver hesitated. "It was kind of a wild ride."

Mirabelle laughed. "Don't worry about that. Poppy and I know the safest route to the sea." She gestured to the white-faced otter tidying up the fish bones.

"You mean you're coming with us?" Franklin asked.

"Of course! With all of us working together, we'll have a nice big raft. Whaddaya say?"

Oliver turned to Franklin eagerly. "A raft with lots of otters will be a lot bigger! Is this okay with you?"

"We'll make sure you stay nice and dry," Poppy added, winking at Franklin.

The dachshund looked surprised. "How'd you know I hate to get wet?"

Poppy chuckled. "It wasn't hard to guess. You kept shaking to get the water off you all through lunch!"

In response, Franklin gave another shake, his floppy ears spraying little droplets everywhere. "If the raft will get us there faster, let's do it!"

"Really?" Oliver exclaimed.

Franklin grinned. "Really."

"Well, what are we waiting for?" Mirabelle clapped her paws. "Let's go!"

20

 **LUCY**

Lucy had never felt so helpless in her entire life.

It was one thing when there was a chance Franklin was still in Kingston. But Olympic National Park was almost a *million* acres of rain forest. Zach had immediately texted Bryson and Alex, and they were going to mention Franklin again during the livestream that morning—as Zach pointed out to Lucy, lots of their subscribers were locals who loved hiking and exploring.

But Lucy knew Zach was only saying that to make her feel better.

"We'll go to Dabob Bay," Zach said, starting the

car. "We can look around the beach where the ferry-boat docked. It's about an hour's drive."

"We don't have to," Lucy said quietly. "That video was yesterday—he's probably far away from that beach by now."

"Or maybe he decided he liked that beach and wanted to hang out." Zach pulled out of the parking lot and turned left. "Come on, Luce. We've gotta at least look."

Lucy nodded but didn't respond. The truth was, she desperately wanted to go to the bay. But she couldn't bear getting her hopes up yet again, only to be let down.

They drove in silence for nearly half an hour. Lucy's phone buzzed, and she read a text from Mom:

SC: *Otter lady's looking great this morning!*
LC: *Yay!*
SC: *Any luck with Franklin?*

Lucy stared at the message and tried to formulate a response. She should send Mom the link to that video, let her see for herself that Franklin was miles and miles away . . . and before she knew it, her eyes had filled with tears.

"Ugh, bridge traffic," Zach said, slowing to a stop. Ahead, Lucy saw the line of cars to cross the bridge was creeping forward at a painfully slow pace. Sighing, Zach closed the maps app on his phone and opened the messages app. "Ah, Bryson texted . . . Oh. Luce." Zach's tone changed, and Lucy glanced up. "It's another video."

Lucy leaned over, straining against her seat belt. "Is it Franklin?"

Zach read Bryson's message out loud. "'Remember Cara and Steph, from that rafting excursion I led last month? They're on a hike this morning, just got to a spot with reception, and texted me this vid—this is nuts!'"

Lucy held her breath as Zach tapped the video and it began to play.

A young woman with close-cropped blond hair grinned at the camera. She was sitting on the edge of a sheer drop, legs over the edge, swinging her hiking boots back and forth. Lucy could just make out a river about twenty feet below. The woman holding the phone was laughing, and then suddenly she cried, "Whoa, look!"

The phone shook wildly, then zoomed in. Lucy saw something big floating down the river, but the camera was too out of focus for her to tell what it was.

"Dude, it's an otter raft!"

"Oh, wow! Ugh, stupid phone, focus already!"

"Wait . . . Oh my god. Cara, look!"

"What?"

"*Look!* There's . . . I swear, I think that's a *dog!*"

"*What?*"

The blurry shape floated past, and right before it disappeared from view, the camera finally focused. The video ended, and Zach and Lucy stared at the last frame. Lucy had seen photos of otter rafts before, but the sight of the furry creatures all clinging together and floating down the river was still amazing.

But nothing could have prepared her for the shock of seeing her dachshund puppy, tongue lolling out and ears flying in the wind, sitting on the otter raft and riding down the river like it was nothing extraordinary at all.

21

FRANKLIN

Franklin had to admit, he was having a great time.

The otters all linked their limbs together in a way that formed what felt like a very sturdy raft. Franklin was careful when he moved around, but none of them seemed to mind a paw on the belly or arm—so long as he avoided their faces. And though his paws and his bottom were a little damp, he stayed dry for the most part.

Oliver and Mirabelle and the others chatted for most of the ride, but Franklin stayed quiet. He was thinking about what would come next, once Oliver was back home. Franklin knew he was very, very far from his own home by now. It seemed like no matter how hard he tried to get back, he just ended up farther away.

But he also knew that Lucy would be looking for him. And maybe she would find him if he stopped moving.

Maybe he needed to *stay*.

The sun was high in the sky, and Franklin was beginning to feel drowsy. But just as his head began to droop, he caught a whiff of something familiar.

"The ocean!"

Oliver's head popped up, his eyes wide. "What? Where?"

"I don't see it, I smell it!" Franklin said, suddenly alert. "We must be close!"

"We are," Mirabelle said cheerfully. "You've got a good nose."

Franklin wagged his tail extra hard until Poppy tapped him on the paw and he realized his tail was smacking her in the face. "Sorry!"

"We're about to go 'round a bend pretty fast,"

Mirabelle called. "There's a nice sandy shore around the side where we can stop. Ready?"

Oliver beamed. "Ready!"

Franklin nodded. "Ready!"

"Here we go!"

22

 OLIVER

Oliver could barely contain his excitement—or his nerves. The raft soared around the bend, and now Oliver could smell the salt water, too, and it smelled so good, so much like *home*, that he felt tears prick his eyes.

The raft slowed, and the otters began to paddle their way to the shore. Franklin hopped off and scurried up to dry sand, giving himself a good shake.

"Am I seeing things, or are there otters way over there?" Mirabelle said suddenly, squinting toward the gray line of the ocean. The sandy shore stretched on for miles, and it took Oliver a moment before he saw them—about three tiny black figures making their way down the beach.

Tiny, *otter-shaped* figures.

Oliver tore his eyes from the otters and looked back at the ocean. He pictured the great mass of land, the one with the towering mountains and lush green forests that seemed so far away from his home. The land that Lulu raved about visiting with her momma.

The land that Oliver was standing on right now.

"Oliver?" came a distant cry of astonishment. "Oliver, is that you?"

"Lulu?" Oliver couldn't believe it. One of the otters in the distance was scurrying toward him, and the closer she got, the more familiar she became. "Lulu!"

Oliver ran as fast as he could, the river otters and Franklin right behind him.

"I can't believe it!" Lulu cried, throwing her arms around him. Oliver laughed as Sammy and Pearl joined them, their eyes wide with amazement.

"How'd you end up here?"

"Last time we saw you, you were swimming toward Puget Sound!"

"Mirabelle!" Lulu cried suddenly, hugging her cousin. "What are you doing here?"

"Giving your friend a lift back to the ocean," Mirabelle said with a grin. "Oliver here showed up at the waterfall earlier today. Sounds like he's had quite the adventure!"

Oliver tried not to blush as Lulu, Pearl, and Sammy stared at him with their mouths open.

"You went to the *waterfall*?"

"In the *mountains*?"

"Yeah," Oliver said, shrugging like it wasn't that big of a deal. "Me and Franklin."

"How'd you get there?" Lulu asked, her eyes shining. "We were so worried you'd gotten lost in the oil spill."

"Oil spill?"

"The black stuff in the water," Lulu said, back to her usual know-it-all tone. "Momma says it's oil."

Oliver swallowed hard. "I did get lost in it. Me and Momma. We got separated, and I woke up on a beach.

She . . ." He didn't want to ask this next part. But he had to. "She made it home . . . right?"

Pearl and Sammy exchanged a look, and Lulu's face fell. "We haven't seen her since she went after you," Lulu said softly. "We thought you two were together."

Oliver stared down at the sand, trying not to cry. He'd managed to stay safe and make it home.

But Momma hadn't.

23

 **LUCY**

The moment Zach pulled into the parking space in
front of Sound Marine Lab, Lucy unbuckled her seat
belt and threw the door open. Mom and Ellen were
by the van, loading a giant crate into the back. Even
from here, Lucy could see the otter was awake—and
very agitated.

"Is she okay?" Lucy asked breathlessly.

"She's a feisty one!" Ellen said with a grunt as they
set the crate down. "But that's a good thing. I'm sure
she's just eager to get home."

"Mom, did you watch the video I texted you?" Lucy
asked.

Mom let out a laugh. "Are you kidding me? Ellen and I watched it about a dozen times, and I still can't believe it. That really did look like Franklin riding on an otter raft!"

"I noticed something else, too," Ellen added. "It's not obvious unless you zoom in, but those weren't all river otters. One of them was definitely a sea otter. Bigger than the others, with a very different build."

"Probably the same one from that juggling video," Mom said, shaking her head. "Franklin's found a buddy, apparently."

"The girls who took the video sent us a map of that location," Zach said, coming up behind Lucy. He held out his phone so Mom and Ellen could see. "This is the river Franklin was on. It goes all the way to Neah Bay."

"Where she's from, right?" Lucy added, pointing to the otter in the crate.

Mom's mouth opened and closed. "Well, yes, we think that's where she's from—that's the biggest community of sea otters nearby. But . . . gosh, that's such a weird coincidence, isn't it?"

Lucy gazed at the otter's furry white face. A wild thought had just occurred to her . . . but no. It couldn't be.

She pictured the two rocks the otter had carried in her pocket, one large and bumpy, one small and flat. She thought about the oily footprints outside the clam shack, about the baby otter eating up all the clams, juggling on the ferryboat, running down the beach with Franklin.

"What if it isn't a coincidence?" Lucy said softly.

Mom, Ellen, and Zach all looked at her.

"What do you mean, hon?" Mom asked.

Lucy swallowed. "Do you have both of her rocks?"

"She has them," Ellen said, nodding to the otter. "I thought she'd just pick one, but she took both and put them in her pocket so fast, it was like she thought I was going to try and steal them."

"Good." Lucy took a deep breath. "Maybe . . . Do

you think maybe it's possible that the baby sea otter with Franklin is her son?"

No one responded. Lucy looked at Mom and Zach, both of them wearing the same expression—kind of stubborn, kind of sad. She took a deep breath.

"The otters washed up on two different beaches, but not very far apart," she pointed out. "I bet that second rock she's carrying belongs to the baby. That's why she's so protective of it, and why she's so worked up. She misses her son. She's worried about him."

Lucy fell silent. For a moment, no one spoke.

"Well, in that case," Ellen said lightly, "we'd better get going. Shall we?"

She closed the back door, then pulled out her keys and headed over to the driver's side. Lucy turned to follow Zach back to his car but stopped when Mom put a hand on her arm. When she looked up, she was startled to see Mom's eyes had filled with tears.

"How about you ride in the van," Mom said quietly. "And I'll ride with Zach."

Zach looked surprised, then wary. "Really?"

Mom nodded, offering him a smile. "It's a long drive. It'll give us a chance to talk."

After a moment, Zach relaxed and smiled back. "Okay, Mom. I'd like that."

He headed to his car, and Mom pulled Lucy into a tight hug.

"Sorry about this morning, sweetie," she whispered. "We'll always be a family, okay? The three of us. I promise."

"Thanks, Mom," Lucy whispered hoarsely.

Mom stepped back, wiping her eyes. "Now, let's go find Franklin, right?"

Lucy nodded. "Right."

She climbed into the van and closed the door, watching in the side mirror as Mom joined Zach. Ellen gave her a knowing smile as she started the engine.

"One reunion down, two to go," she said.

Lucy glanced over her shoulder at the crate in the

back of the van. The otter was squeaking and squawking in agitation.

"It's going to be okay," she told the otter as the van turned out of the parking lot. "Everything's going to be okay."

If she said it enough times, maybe it would be true.

24

 **FRANKLIN**

Franklin felt terrible for Oliver. He hung back as the other sea otters comforted him. The one called Lulu kept saying that Oliver's momma was probably still out there in Puget Sound looking for him.

But Franklin remembered what Oliver had looked like on the bay, all covered in slick black stuff and tired and weak. If Oliver's momma was still in that water . . . The thought made Franklin shudder.

He desperately wanted to make Oliver feel better. Maybe he could find another special rock! Franklin started to scout the beach, making sure not to stray too far from the otters. This beach was much sandier than the others he'd visited, but he was determined to find the perfect rock.

There! A white rock glittered in the sun. Franklin picked it up—it wasn't too big, but it was nice and heavy.

A rumbling noise startled Franklin, and he dropped the rock and whirled around. There was an empty parking lot not too far away—only it wasn't empty anymore. A van had just pulled up, along with a small car. Franklin stared as the van rolled to a stop, and one of the doors flew open.

"Franklin!"

Franklin stared in complete disbelief as Lucy sprinted across the parking lot. Then, with a joyful *"ARF!"* that caused the otters to jump in alarm, Franklin sprinted toward Lucy as fast as his little legs could carry him.

25

 OLIVER

Oliver watched as Franklin leaped into the arms of the girl. She sat down right on the sand and cuddled him close, and Oliver couldn't tell if she was laughing or crying. An older boy was hurrying toward them, and Franklin greeted him with almost as much enthusiasm as he'd greeted Lucy.

"I can't believe you made friends with a dog," Lulu said admiringly. "I've never even *seen* a dog until today!"

Oliver knew she was trying to make him feel better. But as proud of his adventures as Oliver had been moments ago, now he just felt despondent.

"Those people are looking at us," Sammy said, moving closer. "What's that they're carrying?"

The otters all banded together tightly as two women began carrying a big box toward them. There was a racket coming from inside, a scolding squeal that Oliver recognized immediately—but no, that was impossible.

Still, his heart began to pound as the women drew closer.

"That sounds like . . ." Lulu said.

"It really does . . ." Pearl added.

"Is it . . . ?" Sammy wondered.

The women set the box down. Through the bars, Oliver could see a pair of black eyes and a familiar white, furry face. One of the women pulled the door open, and Oliver stepped forward.

"Momma?"

"Oliver!" Olympia cried, and Oliver raced across the sand and threw himself into his momma's arms.

"I knew it!" he heard Lucy say, and Franklin let out an excited *"Arf!"*

Oliver pulled away, so happy he thought he would burst. "Why were you in a box? How did you get here?"

Olympia smiled. "I had quite an adventure. But then again, I think yours might have been even bigger than mine," she added, glancing curiously at the river otters standing with Lulu, Pearl, and Sammy.

"I'm sorry, Momma," Oliver said, guilt washing over him again. "I'm sorry I tried to swim off when you told me not to."

"It's okay, Oliver," Olympia said softly. "I wanted to keep you safe, but I know I've been strict—maybe too strict. It's okay to have a little adventure every now and then." Her expression turned sly. "And I'm very curious to hear all about yours!"

Oliver thought about the wild ride down the river, juggling rocks in front of a crowd on a ferryboat, and facing down a bear. He grinned at Olympia.

"I don't know if you want to hear about *all* of it."

Olympia laughed. "Probably not. Oh, I almost forgot!" Reaching into her pocket, she pulled out—

"My rock!" Oliver cried joyfully, taking it from her. "I thought I'd lost it forever. Franklin kept . . ."

Oliver trailed off, looking over to where Franklin stood next to Lucy. Their eyes met, and Franklin's tail wagged furiously.

"Be right back," Oliver told Olympia, and then he hurried over to Franklin.

Lucy's eyes widened, and she took a step back. The boy stood next to her, holding out one of those flat boxes just like everyone on the ferryboat had when Oliver started juggling.

"Told ya Sarah would be able to find your momma!" Franklin said happily.

Oliver laughed. "You were right! And you'll never guess what she had!"

He held up his rock, and Franklin's eyes widened.

"Your rock?"

"Yup!" Oliver hesitated. Then he held it out. "I want you to have it."

Franklin stared at him. "You do? Why?"

"It's a thank-you present," Oliver said. "For helping

me get home. And . . . and because you're my best friend."

Franklin wriggled with joy. "I am?"

"Yeah!"

The dachshund took the rock carefully in his teeth. Then he set it down on the sand and said, "Wait! I have something for you, too!"

Oliver watched as Franklin darted around Lucy and the boy, then returned with another rock in his teeth. He dropped it into Oliver's outstretched paws.

"I found this one for you before Lucy got here!"

Oliver admired the rock. It had a nice sharp edge and it was surprisingly heavy. It was a little bigger than his old rock, but that was okay. Maybe that was even a good thing.

"It's perfect," he told Franklin, who let out a joyful *"Arf!"*

Two months later . . .

"Franklin? Franklin!"

Lucy stepped out onto the back porch, hands on her hips. A second later, a furry bearded face popped up from behind a bush, and she giggled.

"Franklin, come!" she called, and the dachshund obediently trotted across the backyard and up the porch steps. "Ready to visit your friend?"

Franklin wagged his tail extra hard and scampered across the kitchen. He plucked the flat gray rock off the mat next to his water bowl and returned to sit next to Lucy's feet.

Mom screwed the lid onto her thermos of coffee and smiled. "I think he knows exactly what's going on," she told Lucy.

Lucy grinned as she leaned over to scratch Franklin behind the ears. "Definitely."

The marina was on the south side of Whidbey

Island, a short drive away. Lucy rolled down her window and laughed as the wind blew Franklin's ears straight back. She kept a grip on the back of his harness, but the puppy made no attempt to leap out of her lap.

Fifteen minutes later, Lucy, Mom, and Franklin walked across the marina to where Zach was waiting. "Like my suit?" he joked, turning in a circle with his arms outstretched. He was wearing what looked like rubber overalls that were about two sizes too big.

"Stylish," Mom teased. "I suppose we get to get all dressed up, too?"

"You bet," Zach replied, pointing to the red-and-white boat behind him. The brand-new paint job on the side read ABZ TOURS, and two more pairs of rubber overalls hung over the railing, along with . . .

"Is that a life jacket for Franklin?" Lucy asked.

"Of course!" Zach replied. "Here, I'll put it on him. Can't be too careful—he might decide to take a swim!"

Lucy handed Zach the leash, then grabbed the smaller pair of rubber overalls. "He's gotten really good at *stay*," she told her brother. It was true—Franklin had passed his obedience test with flying colors. But she was grateful that Zach had brought the life jacket, just in case Franklin got a little *too* excited on the boat.

Once they were all seated, Franklin safe and secure in Lucy's lap, Zach guided the boat out of the marina and they set off across the water. It was a chilly, slightly overcast day, and the occasional spray of cool water made Lucy grateful for the bulky rubber overalls. The suits were mandatory for whale-watching tours, because if the boat was close to a whale that actually jumped out of the water, the splash was pretty huge.

It had happened just a few weeks ago. Zach had been leading the tour, while Bryson had been taking video. He'd captured every second of it—the whale leaping from the water, spinning to show its underside before crashing back into the waves and completely soaking the thrilled tourists. The video was the most watched on the ABZ Tours YouTube channel, and Zach's schedule was booked solid through November.

But today was a private family tour. And they weren't looking for whales.

Lucy gazed at the Olympic Mountains taking shape through the misty sky as their boat sped through the strait and headed west toward Salish Sea. She felt for Franklin's rock, which she'd tucked into her pocket for safekeeping during the ride.

"Start keeping an eye out!" Zach called as he cut the engine and pulled out his phone. "They could be anywhere around here."

Lucy hurried to the railing, holding Franklin close to her chest as she gazed out at the water. Mom joined her, while Zach kept watch on the other side.

Suddenly, Franklin wiggled in Lucy's arms.

"Arf! Arf! Arf!"

"Do you see them?" Lucy asked eagerly, staring around. She couldn't see anything but water.

"Maybe he can smell them," Mom suggested. "He's . . . Oh, look!"

She pointed, and Zach hurried over to join them as almost a dozen furry brown heads made their way to the boat, leaving ripples in their wake.

"There he is!" Lucy cried as a familiar otter swam

up to the side of the boat. He waved his little arms, and Lucy could see the chunky white rock Franklin had given him clenched in one paw. Quickly, she pulled the flat rock out of her pocket and gave it to Franklin, who finally stopped barking and took it gently in his teeth.

"And there's the momma otter," Mom said, leaning over the railing and beaming at the white, furry face gazing up at her. "Hello again, little lady. You're looking good!"

"Are you getting this?" Lucy asked as the otter reached up as far as he could out of the water. She held on to Franklin tightly as she leaned over the railing until the puppy and the otter were nose to nose.

"You know it," Zach said, moving closer with his phone. "This is amazing, Lucy."

Standing pressed between her mom and her brother, with Franklin in her arms and a family of otters floating happily around their boat, Lucy couldn't have agreed more.

Acknowledgments

Huge thank you to my editor, Orlando Dos Reis, whose wisdom is as great as any momma otter, and to my agent and resident dachshund expert, Sarah Davies. I'd also like to thank everyone at Scholastic, including Amanda Maciel, Keirsten Geise, Caroline Flanagan, Mary Kate Garmire, Courtney Vincento, Priscilla Eakely, Laura Kennedy, and Emily Epstein White.

And, of course, thank you to all the pets (water-loving or otherwise!) for being better companions than we deserve. If you have a pet, please give them a belly rub from me!

About the Author

Michelle Schusterman is the author of over a dozen books for kids and teens, including *Spell & Spindle*, *Olive and the Backstage Ghost*, and the series The Kat Sinclair Files and I Heart Band. She's also the co-author of the Secrets of Topsea series under the name M. Shelley Coats. She currently resides in Dallas with her husband and their polar bear masquerading as a Lab puppy.